FRIENDS FORNEVER

A Romantic Comedy

MELISSA BALDWIN

Books by Melissa Baldwin

COZY MYSTERY

Killer Couture: A Small-Town Cozy Mystery

Poison in Paradise: a tropical romantic mystery

Movie Scripts & Madness (The Madness and Murder Mysteries #1)

Room Service & Murder (The Madness and Murder Mysteries #2)

∾

ROMANTIC COMEDY

Can't Hurry Christmas: A Holiday Romantic Comedy

Now That We Don't Talk: A Romantic Comedy

All the Christmas Vibes: A Holiday Romantic Comedy

Love in Overtime: A Sweet Small Town Hockey Romcom (Love on Thin Ice Multi-Author Series)

Soulmates and Slapshots: A Sweet Small Town Hockey Romcom (Love in Maple Falls Multi-Author Series)

Can We Talk?: A Romantic Comedy (Question #1)

I Think He Knows?: A Romantic Comedy (Question #2)

A Very Complicated Christmas: A Holiday Romantic Comedy

Unlucky Christmas: A Holiday Romantic Comedy

It Could Happen: A Romantic Comedy

Friends ForNever: A Romantic Comedy

One Way Ticket (written with Kate O'Keeffe)

Thanks for the Love: A Novella (Thankful #1)
Thanks for the Memories (Thankful #2)
Thanks for the Friendship (Thankful #3)

Love and Ohana Drama (Twist of Fate #1
Fate and Blind Dates (Twist of Fate #2)
Glances and Taking Chances (Twist of Fate #3)

On the Road to Love (Love in the City #1)
All You Need is Love (Love in the City #2)
From Runway to Love (Love in the City #3)

Fall Into Magic (Seasons of Summer #1)
Winter Can Wait (Seasons of Summer #2)
To Spring With Love (Seasons of Summer #3)
Return to Summer (Seasons of Summer #4)

See You Soon Broadway (Broadway #1)
See You Later Broadway (Broadway #2)

An Event to Remember (Event to Remember #1)
Wedding Haters (Event to Remember #2)
Not Quite Sheer Happiness (Event to Remember #3)

About Friends ForNever

Erin Taylor is a hard-working journalist with a serious TV addiction and lack of a social life. She's focused on her career and determined to leave her tiny cubicle behind for a fabulous corner office! But when a new co-worker, a friendship drama, and a hot workplace crush collide, Erin finds it harder and harder to focus. Especially when that crush on the oh-so-yummy Aiden Thomas starts to materialize into what feels like a magical relationship. Erin's life seems to finally be heading in the right direction...until suddenly friends aren't such great friends after all, her magical relationship hits a bumpy road, and her career could be derailed by it all. Erin learns a lesson the hard way: Sometimes people aren't who they seem to be. With her happiness on the line, can Erin rise above her disappointments and create the life she's always dreamed of or will she be stuck being Friends ForNever?

"Packed with love, laughter, and deliciously devious frenemies, Friends ForNever is an entertaining romantic comedy for the keeper shelf!"~ Gemma Halliday, New York Times & USA Today bestselling author

To my dearest friends:

Maria—my best friend in Heaven
Betty—my bestie on the West Side
My husband, Chris—my soul mate

Chapter One

*Y*ou've got to be kidding me, not again. I rub my funny bone, and honestly, it's not funny. I try to play it off and pretend like I planned my not so graceful trip, but I'm sure most of the fifth floor witnessed my run-in with the wall. I make my way back to my desk, massaging my latest elbow injury.

"So, do you think I should pursue this dating doctor?" Bre asks as I sit down. "Or do you think doing that's basically saying I'm a loser who can't get her own date?"

Poor Bre, we go through this weekly. Honestly, I don't know why she asks me for dating advice because I wouldn't call myself an expert. I haven't had a decent date since *American Idol* was popular, and everyone knows that hasn't been for several years. I've heard it's been revived, but do people still watch it? Also, this isn't Bre's first rodeo when it comes to these online dating sites.

"I'm sure a lot of people see a dating doctor," I say, trying to appease her.

I sit down at my desk and try to focus on my latest project. I'm hoping that someday one of these articles will catapult me into a better position here at *Strike a Pose* magazine. I'd love to have my name embossed in gold letters on the door of my own office. I can see it now: *Erin Taylor, Assistant Editor* or even better, *Erin Taylor, Executive Editor.* Ha! A girl can dream, but for now, I will sit in my cute little cubicle next to Bre and her many distractions.

"Would you go?" she asks, twisting a strand of her blonde hair around her fingers. "You know, to meet with the dating doctor?"

I shrug my shoulders while nodding my head. *Why not?* At this point I wouldn't have anything to lose. My answer must satisfy her. She holds up her phone and snaps about fifty selfies at all different angles. I really hate selfies. I know it's the thing right now, but for some reason I can't seem to master the art of the selfie. Somehow the photos always turn out awkward and distorted, almost as bad as the camera in the self-check line. Yikes.

I've actually heard selfies can distort your face a bit. I've tried holding the phone up high and tilting it down, but I still think I'm doing it wrong. At least my blue eyes really pop, so I'll count that as a win.

Meanwhile Bre is creating a glamorous photo montage for what I'm assuming is an application or profile for yet another dating page.

Maybe I should check out this dating doctor or whatever he's called. He might be able to give me some advice on how to act around Aiden. Ahhh...Aiden. *Insert a swoony sigh.* I still remember the first time I met him. It wasn't one of my finest moments. I hadn't been with the magazine for very long. Bre and I were rushing back from lunch, and I gracefully tripped on the corner of the hideous shag rug that sits in the corner of our lobby. I landed with my backside in the air right in front of Aiden, and the rest is history. Of course, I immediately started crushing on him. The crush of all crushes—at least the first good one I've had in a while. You're never too old to have a crush right? Twenty-eight is definitely still young.

Don't all women develop a crush on a friend/coworker at some point in their lives? Like most crushes, my interest in Aiden began as a flirtatious friendship and has slowly developed into more, at least on my part.

Bre thinks he's interested in me too, but he's never asked me out. Well, I guess that's not completely true. He did ask me if I was going to our art director's birthday party, but everyone in the office was going, so I didn't want to read too much into it. Normally, I don't blab my personal business around the office, unfortunately Bre caught on to my pathetic attempt at flirting with Aiden. I tried to act innocent and deny it, but I'm a horrible liar. Even if I was a good liar, after having our desks next to each other for a few years, Bre has gotten to know me well enough to know the truth.

"I did it," Bre announces dramatically, interrupting my thoughts. She leans back in her chair as if she has completed some overwhelming task. I pretend I don't hear her and try to get back to work on my latest article.

Aside from Bre and her dating drama, I've had a horrible time concentrating on my work lately. I try to find any excuse I can not to write, and I'm not exactly sure why. That being said, it comes as no surprise when my attention is drawn away from my computer and Bre.

I see Chelsie near the elevator talking animatedly to a girl I don't recognize. Normally, when a supervisor walks in, employees scramble to look like they are actually working, but not our team. I glance around at my wonderful coworkers. Kevin, Mike, and Sean are talking about a new club that opened last weekend, Kimmy is online shopping, Jeannie is on the phone with her feet propped up on her desk, and Bre is scrolling through her phone, probably editing her selfies. Chelsie and the mystery girl start walking toward us.

"I know you're all extremely busy, but can you pry yourselves away from your work for a few minutes?" she asks sarcastically. Everyone looks up at once to give Chelsie their attention. The new girl is sure to create some interest.

"Fifth floor gang, I want to introduce you to your new teammate, Aly Sanders. Aly is a newbie straight out of school, so go easy on her," she warns. "Aly, this is our fantastic writing team. You'll learn a lot from them as I'm sure you can tell."

Everyone ignores Chelsie's comment, and we introduce ourselves to poor Aly, who looks like she's going to puke. Aly is petite with shoulder-length blonde hair and big brown eyes. She seems completely overwhelmed.

When I first started in this industry a few years ago, I was terrified, so I can empathize with how she may be feeling. As much as I wanted to start my career, I longed for those carefree days before real adulting set in. Chelsie shows Aly her new cubicle, which is right across from me.

My friend Jenn used to sit there until she ran off with the circus. Really. Well, maybe not the actual *circus*, but more like one of those traveling carnivals that take up residence in shopping centers during the holidays. We all went one night after work, and she met the guy who controlled the bumper cars. I think they got engaged that night. She quit two days later, and I haven't heard from her since. Bre thinks she joined a cult because she left so abruptly. I had to talk her out of writing an article about it for her gossip column. It would have made a good story, but Jenn was our friend. Anyway, I still wouldn't be surprised if the alleged story of Jenn and some carnival cult surfaced. Bre can be unpredictable.

Chelsie is still talking to Aly, so I wait patiently to introduce myself to her. The rest of the team has already lost interest and returned to their other random tasks.

"Hi, I'm Erin Taylor," I say cheerfully, after Chelsie steps away to answer a call on her phone. "You okay?"

Aly gives me a weak smile. I really hope she doesn't puke because seeing someone throw up will make me throw up, and then we'll have a huge mess on our hands. And with my luck Aiden will show up just in time to see what I had for breakfast.

"Yes, just a bit nervous."

"I totally understand," I reply. "Let me know if you need help with anything."

"That would be so great," she exclaims. "I really enjoy your articles. You're an excellent writer, so I'm sure you'll have plenty to teach me."

I feel my cheeks get hot. I always get a little embarrassed when people compliment my writing, even though it's a huge bolster to my ego, and who doesn't love that.

"Oh, thank you so much."

Chelsie interrupts our conversation and whisks Aly away to continue her tour. She seems like a nice girl and not just because she complimented my writing, although that scored her some points.

"She seems nice," I say when I sit back down in my chair. Bre hardly paid Aly any attention, but that's typical of her. And today she's much too preoccupied with her dating profile to think about the new girl. I sigh as I stare at my laptop waiting for inspiration to strike.

"Psst, ET, you want to grab lunch?" A deep voice asks, startling me. I must've been so enthralled in my attempt at writing that I don't even notice Aiden approach my desk.

I practically jump out of my chair and spin around. He knows I hate being called by my initials, ET, because unlike the majority of the world, I didn't like the friendly alien movie. I know it's supposedly one of the best films of all time, but whatever.

"You know I hate being called that," I say, folding my arms in protest as I pretend to act tough. The truth is—inside I'm dying. I hate the nickname, but I love the attention from him. I try to shift a little, so it doesn't look like I'm staring at his handsome face. His brown hair, structured jawline, and the adorable dimple in his chin. And aside from his dashing looks, he's a really nice person.

"Yeah, yeah. So, lunch?" he asks again.

"Sure," I say nonchalantly. I silently remind myself to stay calm. I'll take any chance to hang out with Aiden that I can.

I save my project on my computer and grab my bag while trying to hide my excitement. My excitement is short-lived, however, when Bre invites herself to crash our lunch all because she needs a man's advice about the dating doctor. I make a promise to myself to never forgive her.

"I don't get it," Aiden says while shoving a handful of french fries in his mouth. "A dating doctor?"

Bre has monopolized most of our lunch with this nonsense. Maybe she forgot about my little crush, because she's basically taken over my romantic lunch with Aiden.

"He has a great reputation," she says defensively. "What about you, Aiden? Would you ever see a dating doctor, or are you already an expert on women?"

He casually leans back. Damn, he's sexy. I try not to stare, as I brush my hand against my chin just in case any drool happens to escape.

"Hell, no. I don't need to get advice from some dude who claims to be the doctor of love."

"Oh really? Well, are you seeing anyone right now?" Bre asks. She throws a subtle side-glance at me.

She's dead to me.

"No, " he says flatly. "But I definitely don't need to pay someone to find a date."

I hope my silence isn't too obvious, but I'm not really sure what to say. Truthfully I'm a little curious to see where this conversation is going.

"Are you sure about that?" she asks.

He bites his lower lip and turns to me. "I'm positive. Watch."

I can tell by the way he's looking at me that he's about to say something important. I'm completely mesmerized by his chiseled face and blue eyes. Honestly, I could stare into his eyes for hours.

"ET, I mean, Erin, would you like to go out sometime? For real, though. Just me and you…not with anyone else," he adds, shooting Bre a smug look. She doesn't seem bothered by it. In fact, she looks quite proud of herself. I may have to forgive her after all.

I smile at Aiden and try to play it cool. "Would I like to go out *sometime?*" I repeat. "When would *sometime* be?"

He cracks a smile. "Oh, you're funny, aren't you? How about next Friday night?"

Is this really happening? Did Aiden finally ask me out?

Bre throws her blonde hair over her shoulder and lets out a

deep sigh as if she's put in a full day's work. I'm impressed—
maybe she should consider being a dating doctor.

"Um, sure. I don't think I have plans," I say casually.

The truth is that I know I don't have plans, other than an
exciting night of catching up on *General Hospital* from the
week. Yes, my life is that uneventful right now, but I'd never
admit it out loud.

"Great," he says just as casually. We smile at each other, and for
a brief few seconds, I forget that Bre is even there.

When we return to the fifth floor, Bre spins around in her
chair a few times. "You can thank me at any time. Go on, tell
me how brilliant I am."

I've been trying my best to hold in my excitement because I'm
about to explode. Not exactly something I want to do in front
of everyone at the office.

"Thank you," I say with a huge grin. "And yes, that was rather
brilliant."

I finally arrive home from work around seven and prepare to
curl up on my couch for a long night of binge-watching *Sex in
the City* reruns. I admit a few of my article ideas have been
inspired by this show, and let's be honest, I think most women
could learn a few things from Carrie Bradshaw. If anything,
I'd love to spend just one night in her closet. Yes, I have a
small TV addiction, but in my defense it's my favorite way to
unwind. My lack of social life doesn't help matters either.

I make a taco salad and finally sit down pulling my feet under me. I look around the room and let out a content sigh. I absolutely love my apartment. The whole building was renovated a few years ago, and it has a stunning view of downtown San Francisco. I got a huge bonus last year and went a little crazy at Pottery Barn, so it's decorated exactly the way I want.

I'm in the middle of one of Carrie Bradshaw's crazy adventures when I pull up my emails on my phone—a decision I immediately regret. Sure enough, there's a message from Chelsie.

Team: Important Mandatory Meeting tomorrow at 3 p.m., and in case you've forgotten—mandatory means everyone needs to attend.

I groan. I love Chelsie, but I don't love her mandatory meetings. They usually turn out to be pointless. They could easily be emails, but I'm not in charge...yet. I may have to come down with a sudden illness tomorrow at 2:55 p.m. Although I'm curious as to why the quick announcement. She usually gives more notice and more explanation. Maybe this meeting is about something important.

I text Bre to find out if she has any idea what the meeting could be about.

Why are you checking emails? Do you ever stop working? We just left the office.

I frown.

Of course, I do.

I stop myself before I say anything else. The fact is that my job is basically the only exciting thing in my life right now.

Other than my surprise evening with Aiden—which I owe to Bre.

Sure you do. I'm sure it's not a big deal. Hopefully, it's a big announcement about us all getting raises.

I smirk.

Let's hope that's it.

When I arrive at the office, Aly is already there, ready for her exciting first day. I look at her desk and raise my eyebrows. It's pretty obvious that she's fresh out of school by the way she's already decorated. She's included a bouquet of fresh flowers, a framed picture of an adorable dog, and a few tiny stuffed animals.

"Good morning," she sings cheerfully.

Poor Aly. Bre is going to have plenty to say about this girl.

"I brought coffee and bagels, so be sure to help yourself."

"Ah, smart move," I tell her as I hang my denim jacket on the back of my chair. "Bringing food will definitely score you some brownie points in this office."

Her shoulders relax. "Good. I hope it doesn't look like I'm trying too hard," she says as she fixes her flowers. I don't have the heart to tell her that it *absolutely* looks like that.

I sit down at my desk and attempt to get back to the article I've been working on for days. I hate to use the term *writer's block*, but I may have a case of it. Of course, Bre's ongoing dating-doctor drama and my impending surprise date with Aiden don't help my concentration.

Aly sits at her desk and pretends to look busy. I'm sure her nerves are out of control right now. It's hard being the new girl, just trying to get settled and not sure what you should be doing. You would think she won the lottery when HR calls her to fill out more paperwork. She practically dances her way to the elevator. Bre finally strolls in, about forty-five minutes late, and immediately lays her head on her desk.

"What's wrong with you?" I ask.

"Nothing's wrong. I was just up late reading about the dating doc's success stories." She lifts her head, a funny look spreading across her face.

"What the hell is that?" she asks, pointing to Aly's cubicle. "Stuffed animals? Are you kidding me?"

I try to hide my giggle. I knew Bre wouldn't appreciate Aly's decor.

"Be nice."

She looks taken back. "I'm always nice."

We both know that's not exactly true. Luckily, she loses interest in Aly's desk quickly, and I return my attention to my laptop. I'm hoping I'll somehow find the power to push past the writer's block.

For as long as I can remember, I've loved writing. I think I first knew I wanted to be a journalist when I was in fifth grade and our class was assigned to come up with ideas for the school paper. I may not have a social life, but I'm good at my job—at least I think I am.

When Aly returns, she seems much more relaxed than she did earlier.

"Good morning, Bre," she says politely. "Did Erin tell you I brought in breakfast? Make sure you help yourself."

Bre shoots me a look, and I pretend I don't notice.

"Uh, thanks," Bre replies.

Aly doesn't seem to pick up on Bre's attitude. Instead, she sits down and slides her chair toward us. "So, can you give me the scoop on everything that goes on here? I really want to make a good impression, and it would be super helpful if I knew the ins and outs of *Strike a Pose*."

Bre willingly jumps into this conversation because she loves any opportunity to engage in some good gossip. I'm half listening, but really, I'm just hoping Aiden will swing by our floor.

The marketing department is a few floors below mine, so he would have to make a special trip up to see me. I just want him to mention our date again because it will reassure me that he really wants to go and wasn't just trying to prove a point to Bre.

Confession—I never used to be this way, but I've become a bit jaded after a series of bad dating experiences.

"I'm so excited for my first mandatory meeting," Aly squeals. "When I was in HR, I overheard some people talking about it. They were saying something about big changes coming."

Bre and I glance at each other. Big changes? That could be good…or not.

"What else did you hear?" I demand. "Do you know who was talking about it?" I've raised my voice so much that I'm almost shouting in poor Aly's face.

Her eyes get big, and she leans back. "I'm sorry. I didn't hear anything else."

Bre laughs. "Just ignore Erin. She lives for these boring mandatory meetings. It's kind of sad. I keep telling her to relax when it comes to this place, but I think she'd sleep here if they let her."

I shoot Bre a dirty look, even though she's not completely wrong. I do love my job, but I'm not excited about the meeting, I'm just really, *really* curious.

"Whatever," I say defensively. "Isn't it time for you to get back to your dating website?"

Bre cracks a smile and grabs her phone.

"Ohhh…that sounds fun. What dating site?" Aly asks eagerly. She slides her chair over to Bre. Crap—the last thing I need is for them to team up. I'll never be able to escape discussions about dating doctors and online websites. I may need to consider moving my desk or figure out a way to get into an office with my name on the door.

~

The day seems to be dragging on very slowly, and I haven't seen Aiden at all. I consider sending him a text, but I don't want to appear desperate. Finally, three o'clock arrives. Between my stupid writer's block and no appearance from Aiden, I need something to distract me. Thankfully, Bre was there to witness him asking me out, or I'd wonder if I imagined the whole thing.

As soon as our team is seated in the conference room, Chelsie begins the meeting with a few announcements. Aly is sitting to my left with a notepad, ready to write down every word Chelsie says. I notice she even wrote the words *Mandatory Meeting* at the top of her paper as well as underlining it twice and dotting the letter *I* with a heart. Bre will tease her to no end if she sees it. Luckily, she's too preoccupied with her phone to even notice anyone else around her. I'm sure dating doctor info is much more exciting than another one of Chelsie's mandatory meetings.

"The reason I called everyone here is to let you all in on some fabulous news."

My heart is racing as I sit up even straighter. I'm literally sitting on the edge of my seat.

"Our sister magazine, *Bleu Amour*, has asked that we collaborate on some projects with them. We'll be sending a team to start working on this, and the project will last about two months."

Bre and I exchange excited looks. While this is a huge opportunity, the best part is that our sister magazine happens to be in the one and only City of Light—Paris. It almost sounds too good to be true.

Chelsie continues, "If you're interested in being a part of this project, you'll need to submit an article. Those who submit will go through a whole new interview process in front of a panel, which will be held in the next two weeks. And it absolutely needs to be your best work because only four people will be selected for the team."

The room is abuzz with everyone talking at once. This is it—a chance to actually take my career to the next level. The competition will be fierce though, and I don't doubt for a second that everyone wants a chance at one of those spots.

When the meeting is over, I make a mad dash back to my desk. I'm determined to prove myself. My coworkers are still in the conference room talking about the announcement, so I have a few minutes of peace and quiet to jot down some ideas.

"Finally, a meeting that was worth the time," Bre says when she and Aly return to their desks. "I need to get to work."

I force a smile. Don't get me wrong. Bre is a great writer, but she spends most of her workday on social media and dating websites. She's hardly dedicated to her job. I have no doubt she sees this as an all-expenses paid trip to Paris, and that's the *only* reason she wants to go.

The energy on our floor has definitely shifted since this morning, and people are actually doing what they're paid to do. I'm really going to have to up my game if I want to stand a chance.

Chapter Two

I'm pouring myself a cup of coffee when I hear my phone buzzing. I'm ecstatic to see that it's a text from Aiden.

ET, are we still on for Friday night?

This is the moment I've been waiting for. Truthfully, I'm a little disappointed that he confirmed via text. What was I expecting? A formal invitation, flowers, diamonds?

I should just be happy it's finally happening.

My best friend, Mia, has always been really creative when it comes to dating. One year she even took the time to freeze water in a heart-shaped pan, and inside was a laminated invitation to her homecoming. When her date melted the heart, the note inside said *Now that you melted my heart, will you go to homecoming with me?* People talked about it for years. Granted, I was never that creative. I may or may not have baked cookies or cupcakes for someone at some point, but that's the extent of my creativity when it comes to potential relationships. *Hmm...maybe that could be part of my problem?*

Anyway, I need to stop pouting and respond to his text. And a text is better than nothing—especially because it's Aiden.

Yes, can't wait.

The office has been a different place since Chelsie's big announcement. It's kind of like the twilight zone. I have worked at *Strike a Pose* for two years and have never seen this much work being done—even when there's a deadline. I think Bre has surprised me the most. She hasn't been on her phone as much as usual—which isn't saying a lot—but she's definitely taking this prospective job seriously.

"So, where has Aiden been lately?" Bre asks, taking a break from pounding away on her keyboard.

Has she been reading my mind?

"Do you know where you're going on your big night out?"

I'm not going to let on that I've been worried about him canceling.

"Is that any of your business, Bre?" Aiden says, startling me. *Why does he always sneak up behind us?*

"It's rude to listen to other people's conversations, Aiden," Bre says shortly. "I need to look out for my girl and make sure you don't bail on her. She'd be devastated."

Ugh. I suddenly feel the urge to crawl under my desk and hide.

"Um, thanks, Bre, but I got this." I stop her before she says anything else to embarrass me.

"Let's take a walk." I grab Aiden's arm and pull him toward the elevator. I'd much rather talk to him without a bunch of eyes on us.

"Sorry about Bre. You know how she is," I say, as soon as we're on the elevator. I'm not sure where we're going, so I just push the lobby button.

He waves his hand. "She doesn't bother me. More importantly, I wanted to talk about Friday night. What would you think about taking a drive to Sonoma?" he asks. "We could just leave from here and make an adventure out of it. A family friend owns a vineyard, and it's spectacular."

What would I think? I think I could die happy.

"That sounds, um...amazing," I answer as I begin to imagine how perfect this night could be.

"Good." He smiles as he inches closer to me. "I'm really looking forward to it. And don't give Bre's nonsense a second thought."

"Okay," I say softly, as I try to remain calm with our close proximity. If we were any closer, we'd be touching, and I wouldn't be mad about it. Our faces are now a few inches apart, and my heart starts to race at the thought of Aiden's lips on mine. Unfortunately, the elevator door opens making us both jump—a few people join us, and the typical elevator silence begins. Aiden and I exchange a few flirty glances, and I'm regretting hopping on the elevator to have this little chat. Duh, a secluded hallway would have been a much better option. Although I had no idea we'd almost kiss. I'll never make this mistake again, that's for sure.

When we stop at the lobby, the two people who intruded on our moment leave, but Aiden and I stay on the elevator. The door closes, and we're alone again.

"So, I guess we should get back to work," I suggest.

"Yeah, we probably should," he agrees. The elevator sails back to his floor and the door opens.

"I'll see you Friday." Aiden says, as he steps off the elevator. Before the doors shut, he holds his hand out to keep it open. "We can continue our conversation then." He gives me a coy smile.

"Sounds good," I say, my pulse picking up speed once again.

After the door closes, I clap and twirl around excitedly. I have no complaints about continuing what almost happened in the elevator.

I practically float back to my desk, and I must have a silly lovestruck look on my face because Aly and Bre are staring at me.

"What happened to you?" Bre asks suspiciously. "And don't say nothing because I can see it all over your face."

I really want to tell her. Actually, I want to jump onto my desk and announce how I'm feeling to the world.

"Nothing *happened* to me. Aiden and I just took a walk to talk *privately*." I make a point to emphasize that, but knowing Bre, she won't take my obvious hint.

"You guys make such a cute couple," Aly squeals. Bless this girl. I knew I liked her. And I definitely could get used to Aiden and I being a couple.

"Thanks, but Aiden and I are just friends," I reply, trying to sound nonchalant. This is the truth, at least for now.

"What Erin's trying to say is that they aren't a couple *yet*," Bre says, barely looking up from her computer. I'm not sure how I feel about her being so involved in my personal life, but she's right. We aren't a couple yet and I'm hoping that changes after Friday.

"Let's go out for drinks after work," Bre says, quickly turning around in her chair. "We should celebrate the announcement. You in?"

Before I have a chance to respond, Aly speaks up. "I love that idea. How about sushi?"

Bre looks at me and raises her eyebrows. I'm not sure if she was inviting Aly, but it's too late now. And there's no reason we can't include her.

"Oh, why not," I reply.

I glance at Aly, who has a huge smile on her face. "I'm so excited," she squeals.

An evening out with Bre and Aly. This ought to be interesting.

A few hours later, Bre, Aly, Kimmy, and I are seated around a table, drinking wine and laughing. Kudos to Bre for making this suggestion. It's a nice change from my TV binge watching and my workaholic writer's block. Even with Bre's constant babbling about online dating, I'm still having a great time.

"This is so fun, " Aly says. "I knew I was lucky to find an amazing job, but I had no idea I would make friends as well." She holds up her wine glass again. I'm not sure how many glasses she's had because this isn't her first toast of the night. In her defense, starting a new job is incredibly stressful. She probably needed to unwind a little.

I see Bre and Kimmy whisper to each other, and I poke Bre on the arm. "Be nice." Even though I'm not exactly sure they're whispering about Aly, it doesn't hurt to remind her.

"So, Erin, tell us about this hot night you have planned with Aiden," Kimmy says, changing the subject. I give Bre a look. She has the biggest mouth ever. She shrugs her shoulders, clearly trying to claim innocence.

"What hot night?" I ask, taking a long sip of my wine, or rather finishing the glass. I know I don't have a chance in hell of leaving this restaurant without having a discussion about Aiden and me.

The girls are staring at me, patiently waiting for my answer.

"We have more important things to talk about, like the Paris project. Trust me, that's more exciting than my personal life."

Paris has been a hot topic all day, so I'm hoping they'll fall for my suggestion.

"Uh-uh, don't try to change the subject," Kimmy says, holding up her hand. "Everyone knows you and Aiden have wanted each other for a while now. It was just a matter of time before you would finally get together, right, Bre?"

Bre nods her head without taking her eyes off her phone. "And when you get married, you can tell everyone how you owe it all to me."

Married? What? I wave a heat flashes over my body, and I start to sweat.

"Whoa, slow down," I say, holding up my hand. "Aiden and I have been friends for a while, and we enjoy each other's company. And he's making all the plans, so I don't have any more details."

I feel satisfied with my answer. "Now back to the project. What are your thoughts?"

Kimmy and Bre start talking at once about the project and what a huge opportunity it could be for the future. My brilliant plan worked. I notice that Aly has gotten really quiet. She probably doesn't think she has a chance going up against the rest of us who've been in the industry longer. The reality is that she has just as much of a chance as any of us, maybe more. She probably has fresh, new ideas and might be the perfect addition to the team.

The conversation somehow shifts to French food and all the must-see sites to visit in Paris. Don't get me wrong, I want to soak up every bit of culture I can while I'm there, but I'm especially excited about the experience of working abroad. A project like this would look fantastic on my résumé, and it might get me even closer to that coveted office with my name on the door.

"Can you imagine all the European men we could meet?" Bre exclaims, her eyes gleaming. And there it is—I knew it was only a matter of time until she brought up the men.

Aly finally speaks up after what seems like several minutes of silence. "I would just love the experience," she exclaims. "The chance to work on an international project so early in my career would be life-changing. Not many people get this kind of an opportunity—so it's probably not likely that I'll be selected." Her face immediately falls.

"Aly, you have just as good of a chance as any of us. We all have to go through another interview process, so you never know," I remind her.

Bre and Kimmy exchange glances.

"I guess," Aly says, sounding unconvinced.

"Honestly, everyone has to start somewhere in this industry," I add. "I can remember many moments when I thought I was just wasting my time, but every chance I took gave me more and more experiences. Don't you guys agree?" I ask Kimmy and Bre.

Bre doesn't say anything, but Kimmy immediately speaks up.

"I agree," she says. "If I never sent over samples of my work, who knows what I'd be doing right now."

Aly and Kimmy start chatting about my pep talk, and Bre remains preoccupied with her phone as usual. I glance curiously around the room when someone catches my eye at the bar. I let out a quiet gasp when my eyes land on Aiden. I run my fingers through my hair just in case he happens to see us. My heart continues to beat faster, and I take a few deep breaths. Maybe he won't even see us or—

"Is that Aiden?" Bre asks loudly. I'm pretty sure her tone increases several octaves when she drinks.

"What? Where?" I ask, pretending to be surprised that Aiden could possibly be in a restaurant around the corner from our office building.

"Aiden?" she yells. "Aiden?"

Several people turn to look at us. Damn, she's loud.

"Bre, stop yelling," I plead. But her loud calls do the trick and get Aiden's attention. He turns around and waves as soon as he sees us.

I lean back casually my chair as I try to try to hide my joy.

Aiden turns back to the bartender and then starts talking to another very attractive man sitting next to him at the bar. He points to us, and now the other man is waving. A few seconds later, they walk toward us.

"Who's the dreamy guy with Aiden?" Bre asks in a loud whisper. She quickly checks her makeup in her phone.

"Please don't embarrass me," I whisper to Bre.

She flashes me a wicked smile. "Who me?"

"Well, well, what's going on here?" Aiden asks playfully as soon as he approaches our table. "Are we interrupting ladies' night out?" He places his hands on my shoulders, causing an electric shock to shoot through my body.

"You sure are," Bre replies. "But we might let it slide—if you introduce your friend."

She gives the friend a coy smile. "Where are Aiden's manners?"

Kimmy and Aly haven't said anything. They're both staring at the friend, and I can't blame them.

"Yeah, bro. You're being rude," he says slapping Aiden on the back. "Good evening, ladies. I'm Harry, Aiden's charming, better-looking brother."

Brother? Ah yes, they have the same eyes and smile.

"Yeah, and *older*," Aiden adds with a snicker.

The girls are still staring at Harry, and I'm not doing much better. He's a bit more muscular and rugged than Aiden. He also has a few more wrinkles around the eyes, but their smiles are identical.

We go around the table to introduce ourselves. Harry shakes each of our hands firmly. Granted, he has to pry his hand out of Bre's tight grasp.

"You all work at the magazine?" Harry asks. "Damn, maybe I should get a job there. Aiden never told me that his coworkers were so beautiful," He flashes a brilliant smile. Oh, he's smooth, and the girls are practically swooning.

"I just started at *Strike a Pose*," Aly says sweetly. "But everyone has been so welcoming to the new girl."

She bats her eyes at Harry, while Bre glares at her. Aly is more subtle than Bre, but she's not backing down. This should be interesting.

"So tell me, I'm dying to know what it's like working with my little brother." He sits down in a chair that has somehow magically appeared. I look at Aiden, who also finds a chair and sits down. Where did those chairs come from? Have I also become completely mesmerized by Harry's charm and charisma? Aiden subtly slides his chair closer to mine, making my heart do a flip-flop.

"He's annoying as hell," Bre announces. "The only reason he comes around us is to flirt with our ET." She points at me while Aly and Kimmy laugh.

"Oh, I haven't heard about the ET thing yet," Aly says. She's trying extra hard to become a part of our team, and I've been in her corner up until now—but the nickname might be a deal breaker.

I poke Bre on the arm.

"ET?" Harry asks with a smirk on his face.

I raise my eyebrows at Aiden. "Would you like to explain the nickname?"

Aiden slides his arm along the back of my chair. His touch causes my pulse to pick up. "I call her ET, short for Erin Taylor, and she hates that movie."

"What?" Harry exclaims. "What's wrong with you, woman? Nobody hates *E.T.* It's a classic."

Before I have time to respond, the conversation changes to a discussion about the greatest movies of all time, E.T. being one of them. Aiden is sitting to my right, and every so often he will touch my arm or leg or lean toward me. It takes every ounce of strength not to wrap my arms around his neck and kiss him. I'm growing more excited about our evening together with every subtle gesture he makes.

"Sorry we interrupted your girls' night," Aiden whispers.

I shrug my shoulders. "It's fine. Watching the girls flirt with your brother is definitely more entertaining than gossip or listening to Bre talk about the dating doctor."

"This is nothing," he says, pointing to my three friends hanging on Harry's every word.

Hmmm...I get the feeling that Harry is quite the ladies' man.

"So you're saying that women are constantly throwing themselves at him?" I ask. "I suppose you look up to your big brother then?"

Wow, did I just say that? Gah, come on, Erin.

He gives me a curious look. "Nah, I'm definitely a one-woman type of guy."

I think my heart skips a beat. This might be the best girls' night I've ever been to thanks to the Thomas brothers crashing it. I don't know how I'm going to survive until Friday.

It's officially the longest week ever. Every day feels like *Groundhog Day*, and I'm starting to wonder if Friday is ever going to come. Running into Aiden and Harry at the restaurant made it a little more bearable. And I'm pretty sure none of the girls minded their interruption.

Harry ended up getting most of the attention, and I have no doubt that Bre has set her sights on him. Although she may have to battle Aly for his affections. Bre didn't care for Aly before meeting Harry, and now they're on the brink of fighting over the same guy. Which of course will leave me to referee should it come to that.

"Thanks again for your help yesterday," Aly says, pulling me from my daydream. "I'm feeling more settled now that I have an understanding about how the magazine is run."

"Of course," I reply. "Like I told you, I've been in your shoes, so I'm happy to help anytime."

I like Aly, and I guess that's why I've taken her under my wing. I've gone out of my way to make her transition smoother, including walking her through our procedures, introducing her to almost everyone on staff, and most importantly, sharing some insider details about *Strike a Pose*. I remember what it was like to be new, and I wish someone had shown me the ropes of the magazine business. And if mentoring the newbie helps me look good, then that's an extra bonus.

"I have a brilliant idea," Bre says as soon as she sits down at her desk. I haven't had a sip of coffee yet, so I'm not sure I have the strength to deal with one of her ideas this early. "Maybe you could talk to Aiden about Harry and I joining you on your date? The four of us in Sonoma together would be a blast," she exclaims.

What? She can't be serious. She knows how long I've wanted to go out with Aiden, and now she wants to join us.

"So, will you talk to him?" she begs.

Hmm…Bre doesn't like not getting her way, but I have no intention of letting her crash our evening. *Sorry, Bre—not a chance.*

"Um...I'll mention something to him, but I'd really like to have him all to myself this time..."

"Shhhh," she interrupts me, putting her finger up to her lips. I give her a questioning look then I realize Aly has just walked in.

"Good morning," Aly sings, she's practically dancing around the office. *How much caffeine has she consumed?*

"You're chipper this morning. How many cups of coffee have you had?"

She laughs. "Why does everyone ask me that? I actually don't drink coffee."

"Really?" I ask.

"I make my own hot water-lemon detoxifying drink and do yoga, Pilates, or run in the mornings. It's an amazing way to start the day."

I'm completely exhausted by what she just said—something about detox and yoga?

"Anyway," Bre says, ignoring Aly. "Let me know what Aiden says."

She's actually serious. I can't believe she wants to crash our date, not to mention we don't even know if Harry has any interest in her.

Bre's phone rings, and she hurries toward the elevator while answering it. It's obvious she doesn't want us to listen in on her conversation. I let out a heavy sigh and quickly turn toward my desk.

"Hey, Erin," Aly calls.

Ugh. I don't know how I'm going to get any work done with these two and their constant interruptions.

"What's up?" I ask trying not to sound irritated. Maybe I should lock myself in a bathroom stall with my computer.

"Sorry. I know you're trying to work. I was just wondering if you could do something for me." She stops and clears her throat. Ugh, here we go. I have a feeling I'm not going to like this.

"Maybe," I reply.

"I know you have your big night with Aiden coming up, but I was wondering if you could get the scoop on Harry for me."

I should've known.

"Um, I'll see what I can find out," I lie. Despite what these women think, I'm not going to spend my first evening with Aiden playing matchmaker for his brother.

A few minutes later Bre returns from her phone call, but thankfully there's no more mention of Harry or double dates for the remainder of the day.

When I finally get home, I practically fall onto the couch because I'm so exhausted. Before I left work, I ate two peanut butter cookies and a bag of salt and vinegar chips, so I'm not hungry for dinner. I stretch out and pull a fluffy blanket over my lap. I'm just about to doze off when my phone rings. Without moving from the couch, I reach into my bag and grab my phone.

"Hello?"

"There you are. Don't you think it would be nice if you'd call your mother once in a while?"

I groan. "Hi, Mom."

"Where have you been?"

I give her the standard apology complete with the *I've been so busy* spiel.

My mother and I have an interesting relationship. She's always had high expectations of her children, and although I've excelled in my career, my lack of relationship status really stresses her out. My brother is a successful lawyer, has a perfect wife and two adorable children. All of that added together makes him the favorite child. I have yet to live up to her expectations, or at least it feels that way.

"Busy or not, you should always call your mother," she replies. "How would you know if I got sick or kidnapped?"

I roll my eyes because this isn't the first time I've heard this lecture.

"Okay Mom," I exclaim.

"Anyway, I have some wonderful news," she says changing the subject. "I've found the perfect man for you. When can I arrange a meet up?"

Sigh. This isn't the first blind date that she's tried to set me up on. I actually have a semi-long list of excruciating dating experiences thanks to her.

"Mom, I told you no more. I've had enough blind date torture for one lifetime."

She's conveniently forgotten about the last guy she tried to set me up with. He was her neighbors' son, and she insisted he was perfect for me. I noticed all throughout dinner that he was very flirtatious with our server. He even went as far as to ask her to join us on our date after she got off work. Needless to say, I walked out of the restaurant leaving my crème brûlée untouched.

"Erin, it was one bad night. This one is good. I feel it in my gut."

Ugh. She says that every time. Of course, I could get her off my back if I tell her about my date with Aiden. But if I do that, I'll have to deal with the nonstop phone calls and texts about what I'm going to wear and how to do my hair.

"Honey, don't you think it's about time you got into a serious relationship? You're almost thirty," she says, as if my life is nearly over. "Everyone I know is asking me if you're seeing anyone. What am I supposed to tell my friends?"

Really, *everyone* she knows. I twist a pillow in my hand and throw it across the room. She continues to ramble as I pry myself off the couch and stumble to the kitchen. I'm in desperate need of a glass of wine, or possibly a bottle depending on how long this conversation goes.

"Mom, I'm sure your friends don't care about my love life. And in case you've forgotten, I'm twenty-eight, not *almost* thirty," I insist. I pour myself a glass of Pinot Noir and head back to my couch. On second thought, I grab the bottle in my other hand while cradling the phone in my neck.

"That's where you're wrong, Erin. My friends love you like you're one of their own. They want you to be happy."

Huh. What am I supposed to say to that?

"Okay, I promise as soon as I become seriously involved with someone, I'll let you know so you can post it on Facebook."

She chuckles. I'm glad she finds this funny.

"So, does that mean you'll give Wilbur a chance?" she asks.

Wilbur?

"Is that really his name?" I ask.

"Erin, be nice. You can't afford to be picky about a man's name."

I foresee this bottle of wine draining fast. I'll do anything to get off the phone, so I tell her she can give Wilbur my phone number. That doesn't mean I have to go out with him.

I'm deeply immersed in a rerun of *Gossip Girl* when my phone rings again. I really don't want to answer it in case it happens to be Wilbur, or even worse, my mother again.

My stomach fills with butterflies when I see Aiden's number on the screen. I sit up so fast I get dizzy.

"Hello."

"What's up, ET?"

I scowl.

"Hey," I say casually, well as casually as I can. I'm glad he can't see me because I'm sure I look ridiculously happy to hear his voice despite the stupid nickname.

"So, I'm apologizing in advance, but my brother won't get off my back."

His brother? What's with this guy? I feel like he's taking over my life.

"Wait, let me guess," I interrupt. "He wants us to set him up with someone?"

I wonder which girl he's interested in.

"Yes," he exclaims. "How did you know?"

I tell him about Bre and Aly both begging me to talk to him about Harry.

"Well, is he interested in Aly or Bre?" I ask finally. Either way it puts me in a terribly awkward place.

"That's the problem, he says he was intrigued by both of them. My brother is so annoying."

What? Is he joking? He wants to get to know both of these women and throw Aiden and me in the middle.

"Both of them," I exclaim. "There's no way in hell Bre would go for that."

He laughs. "I know. What should we do? Maybe I'll just tell him they're both unavailable."

"Hah, Bre will never forgive you," I tell him. "I think you should give him both of their numbers and let them hash it out. *We* shouldn't have to worry about it."

In other words, I don't care.

"Brilliant idea, ET. May the best woman win."

I smile to myself.

"So, we're set for Friday?" I ask, casually changing the subject to what's more important.

"Definitely. I'm really looking forward to it," he says. I can almost hear him smiling.

"Me, too."

When we get off the phone, I feel exhilarated. Only one more day to go, and I refuse to let my friends' drama ruin this night for me. I've waited much too long for this.

Chapter Three

*F*riday is my favorite day of the week, and not just because I'm going out with Aiden. Although that's definitely a bonus.

I wake up early and don't even hit snooze four times like I usually do. I'm eager to get my day started and hopefully make some progress on my article for the Paris project. Yesterday, I moved to the conference room so I could concentrate. It was a gloriously peaceful day even though I didn't make as much progress as I was hoping too. I'm second guessing every idea I have, which is making me more anxious about my writer's block. Meanwhile Bre called in sick, and Aly isn't bold enough to wander around looking for me. Admittedly I'm a little curious to find out if Harry reached out to either of them, but I don't want to bring it up.

I'm not surprised when I get a text from Wilbur, who thankfully goes by Will. Apparently, my meddling mother told him I love sushi, so of course he asked if I'd like to join him for sushi sometime. I haven't texted him back yet. I consider deleting the text, but my mother's incessant nagging will never let me get away with it.

When I get to the office, Bre is bragging that she finished her article and she's ready for the interview. I can't believe she's done already. I've changed my idea three times, and I'm still not satisfied with it.

"Hey, girl. Are you feeling better?" Aly asks as soon as she arrives. "I thought you and Bre were both sick."

How do I tell her that I went into hiding to avoid her?

"No. I'm fine."

"Oh, well, I have some exciting news," she says. She looks like she's about to explode if she doesn't say something. "I decided to take your advice. I'm going to submit an article for the international project." She barely takes a breath. "Do you think I'm crazy? Tell me the truth."

Huh, for a second I thought she was going to tell me that she spoke to Harry.

"Not crazy at all," I reply. "Like I said, you have just as much of a chance as anyone else."

She looks relieved.

I throw myself into my writing even though it feels like I'm watching the clock constantly. Surprisingly the day flies by with minimal interruptions and finally, it's time to get ready. I brought a change of clothes—a pair of dark skinny jeans with an off-the-shoulder sweater and black booties, as well as my makeup and my flatiron. The office bathroom has practically turned into a salon. I look in the mirror and let out a deep sigh. Normally, I'm pretty content with how I look, but I'm extra uptight since I've been out of the dating game for a while. My mother's voice tends to creep into the back of my mind during moments like this. I'm being totally ridiculous since Aiden sees me at work almost every day. I study my reflection for a few more seconds, run the flatiron through my light brown hair one more time, and add some fresh mascara, bronzer, and lipstick.

My nerves are about to take over, when Kimmy comes into the bathroom. "Damn, girl, you look amazing."

I look around the bathroom at the primping tornado I've caused. I was really hoping everyone had gone home for the day.

"Thanks," I say. "It's not too much, right?"

"Not at all," she insists. "Have fun tonight."

Seriously, you'd think this was my first date ever. And it's Aiden, the same man who teases me with a silly nickname.

I finally head back to my desk, and as I expected, everyone has left. I sit down and make myself look busy while I wait for Aiden. I check my phone and see a text from him.

Be up there in 10.

I start to imagine how the events of the evening could go. We'll start with a delicious dinner, tour of a winery, maybe a picnic under the stars, maybe some hot, passionate kissing and...

"What's going on in that brain of yours?" Aiden asks, pulling me out of my very vivid daydream.

I can feel my face get hot. There's no chance in hell I'll tell him what I was just thinking about.

"What do you mean?" I ask with a nervous laugh. "I was just thinking about, um...this article I'm working on. It's been kind of hard to concentrate."

He gives me a questioning look as he pulls Bre's desk chair over toward me. "Hard to concentrate? Why?"

His close proximity makes me shift around in my chair. I'm not telling him that I've been counting down the days until this moment. Of course, there have been other distractions, but tonight has been the biggest one.

"Just a lot of pressure right now, you know, with the international project and stuff." I stare at his face. *Damn, he's so handsome.*

"Anything I can help with?" he asks, his voice low and smooth. He leans forward, resting his forearms on his legs.

My mind begins to wander as I breathe in his yummy masculine scent. Hmm...I could think of a few things.

"Um, I'm not sure, but I'll definitely let you know," I say, my voice barely above a whisper.

Our eyes are locked on each other, and it seems pretty clear that we're on the same page when it comes to our attraction. Although I definitely don't want our first kiss to be at my desk at *Strike a Pose* magazine.

"I'm ready when you are," I say, not letting go of his gaze.

"Yes, let's do this." He rises to his feet, holding his hand out to me.

I gladly put my hand in his and let him lead me toward the elevator. This night is already off to a perfect start.

I'm having the best time and we haven't even arrived at our destination yet. Other than Aiden calling me ET a few times, he has been perfect. His subtle gestures are everything—like reaching over to touch my arm or pushing a piece of my hair out of my face. I hope he couldn't hear my heartbeat because it felt like it was going to beat out of my chest.

"Okay, my turn to ask a question," he says boldly. I've been talking so much he's barely had a chance to get a word in.

"Sorry," I say, putting my hand to my face.

"Don't apologize," he says, placing his hand on my knee. Another powerful electric shock pulses through my body from his touch. This could be a really good thing or a really bad thing. I wait for him to remove his hand, which thankfully he doesn't.

"Ask me anything you want," I say, moving my hand on top of his. I'm definitely feeling more and more relaxed by the minute.

"Are you close to your family?" he asks. "You've already met my brother, so you know what I have to deal with at family events."

I giggle. "Well, he must not be that bad considering he has two gorgeous women fighting over him right now."

He nods. "True."

"My family is interesting," I hesitate. "Of course I love them, but they can be frustrating, too. My parents divorced two years ago, which was a huge shock for all of us. As you can imagine, after almost forty years of marriage, no one saw it coming. Thankfully they get along really well, so that makes it easier on the rest of us. My dad is retired and plays golf or goes fishing almost every day. My mom is also retired and spends all her extra time going to social events and meddling in my personal life. My brother is a partner at his law firm, is married to Liza, who's as perfect as you can get, and they have the cutest kids. Eric has always been good at everything he does. The guy that never studied but still had the perfect GPA. Everything he touches turns to gold, and my mother thinks he walks on water."

Hmm...hopefully I didn't sound too jaded while describing my family. I do love them all, even my brother.

"So, do you consider yourself the black sheep of the family?" he asks with a laugh. He moves his hand from my knee and takes hold of mine.

Aiden's holding my hand. I feel like a giddy teenager, and for a brief moment, I can't even remember what we were talking about.

"What?" I ask absently. "Oh, I mean, no. Not the black sheep exactly. It's just that everything has always come easy to Eric. I've had to work a little harder to get where I am."

"I know how that is," he says. "Harry is always whining about me being our parents' favorite." He turns his eyes away from the road and gives me a wink.

"Hey, I'm not whining." I punch him in the arm with my free hand. My other hand still comfortably in his.

Before I know it, we pull up at The Bristow Winery. Aiden tells me to wait a second while he runs around to open my door. He reaches in to take my hand and pulls me gently out of the car. As soon as I step out, our lips are closer than ever. My heart speeds up, and I suck in a breath. I must be completely distracted by our locked gazes because my heel gets caught on the edge of the curb, and I start to fall forward. Thankfully, Aiden comes to my rescue by catching me and helping me get steady on my feet.

"Ta-da," I say through my embarrassment. "And my clumsiness makes an appearance."

"Very graceful." He grips my hand firmly as he leads me toward the entrance.

I really couldn't ask for a better start to this evening.

Our table is set up outside, and the scenery is perfect with the green rolling hills and the pink sunset as the backdrop.

Aiden is so warm and attentive. We don't run out of things to talk about, and there isn't an ounce of awkwardness between us. I'm sure being friends first has helped us to be more comfortable with one another.

"So, what do you think about this international project?" I ask after the server clears our plates. The food was so good, it probably looked like I hadn't eaten in days. Honestly, I'm not really a salad and glass of water type of date.

"I think it's exciting," he exclaims. "It's going to be tough competition. I'm not looking forward to the interview process."

Interview process? What's he talking about?

"Wait. What are you not looking forward to?" I ask nervously. "Are you applying for one of the positions?"

He laughs.

"No, I've been asked to be on the interview panel," he explains. "They wanted a diverse group of people making the final decision. I just happened to be the lucky one to be asked from the marketing department. Believe me, I don't want to do it."

Ugh, this could get complicated. *Why does he have to be on the panel?*

"You're planning to interview, aren't you?" he asks.

"Definitely," I reply. "This is an opportunity I've been hoping for my whole career."

He nods in agreement.

"Have you thought about staying here?" he asks curiously.

What? Why on earth would he ask me a question like that?

"No, why," I exclaim. I rub my arms to warm up a little as I can feel the temperature dropping. And just then, Aiden magically produces a fuzzy blanket from under the table and wraps it around me. Seriously, this man has thought of every detail.

"Where did the blanket come from?"

He gives a shrug. "It's all part of the experience."

I could get used to this kind of treatment. And I'll never turn down a blanket.

"I was just thinking that it seems like everyone is so quick to jump on board and they aren't considering the opportunities that'll still be here." He pauses. "You know what I mean? Like in the long term."

Hmm...I never thought about that. The project is two months long. Staying might give me more chance to shine here, but then again, so could an opportunity abroad.

"Bre is applying for it also," I tell him. He nearly chokes on his wine.

"What?" he snorts. "Why would she do that?"

I give him a look that basically says *Why do you think?*

"Well, that's one interview that should be entertaining," he says.

"She's already finished her article, and she claims she's ready to head to Paris."

He rolls his eyes.

"I'm surprised she's still at *Strike a Pose*," he exclaims.

Hah. There've been many times I've thought the same thing—especially those days when she takes extra-long lunches or spends hours researching the dating doctor.

"When Bre applies herself, she's a really good journalist," I tell him.

"I guess," he says doubtfully.

The server brings our dessert, and I take a small bite of my cheesecake. Aiden looks at me and smirks.

"What?"

He reaches over and brushes a tiny bit of whipped cream off my lip with his finger. Neither of us says anything, and without any hesitation, he leans in and kisses me.

Finally! The kiss is tender and slow, lasting only a few seconds but feels like so much longer. He pulls away and smiles.

"ET, I have a confession to make," he whispers.

I'm so mesmerized that I don't even care about the nickname. "What's that?"

He takes a deep breath. "I've been wanting to kiss you for a very long time."

I feel my face light up at his admission.

"Me, too," I say softly. "I mean, I've wanted to kiss you also."

"I'm glad to hear that." He's still whispering, and our faces are still only inches apart. "So does this mean we can go on a second date?"

"I'll think about it," I tease.

Without another word his lips are on mine once again.

Chapter Four

*I*t's Saturday morning, and I'm still lying in bed, remembering every second of my night with Aiden. I'm in such a good mood, which thankfully should help me get through the day. A day with my family.

Unfortunately, I'm kind of dreading going to my niece Kylie's birthday party. I have to be mentally prepared to endure my mother's attempts to set me up with unattached party guests in case her plans for Wilbur and I don't come to fruition. In addition, I'll get to hear all about Eric and Liza's home renovations and recent trip to London. I haven't decided if I should tell them about Paris just yet. Especially because it's not a done deal until after I have my interview and I'm selected for the team.

I take my time getting out of bed, finally getting up to make coffee and then curling up on the couch with my laptop. I don't turn the TV on, which is a huge step for me. Instead, I open my document and write. Maybe going on a date was good for me. I'm sure having a social life will help with my TV addiction. Not that one date counts as a social life, but it's a start, and he did ask me out on a second one.

Before I know it, I completely lose track of time, and it's time to get ready for the party. That's the end of my leisurely Saturday. Let the family fun begin.

On my way to my brother's home, I try to remember the last time I saw him and his family. It's probably been several months and definitely before their London trip. I shouldn't complain too much because I actually really like my sister-in-law, Liza. She's a wonderful wife and mother, not to mention creative, beautiful, and super fit. Basically the whole package. She's always treated me like her own sister, and honestly she's only annoying when she's around my brother. And I absolutely adore my niece, Kylie, and nephew, Knox.

When I pull up in front of their gorgeous home, I can tell the party is already in full swing. There are luxury cars lined up all around the circular drive. The front porch is decorated with a massive balloon arch and a pink birthday banner. From the side of the house, I can see a huge princess-castle bounce house in the backyard and already hear the joyful cheers from the party guests. Admittedly, I love a good bounce house.

I let myself into the grand entry hall. The house is quiet, and I'm assuming most of the guests are outside on the deck. When I walk into the kitchen, I find Liza and her mother organizing platters of food. Liza is wearing a long, flowing maxi dress, and she looks as if she just stepped out of a salon.

"Hey," I say cheerfully.

"Erin," Liza exclaims. She hurries over and throws her arms around me. "Oh, Kylie's going to be so excited. She's been asking for Aunt 'Ewin' all morning."

Liza's mother washes her hands and gives me a hug.

"Good to see you, honey," she says. "You look lovely."

Liza's mom is just as sweet and perfect as she is.

I glance out through the open French doors and see my brother by the bounce house, sitting with the other dads. My mom is draped across a lounge chair by the pool, chatting with a few women. She looks like she's basking in all the glory of her son's nearly perfect life.

"How have you been, Erin? I feel like we haven't seen you in forever," Liza says, arranging vegetables on a tray.

She hasn't seen me in forever.

I sit down at one of her fancy leather barstools. Wow, these chairs are nice—I might need to get some for my kitchen.

"I've been great, just very busy at work." I decided against disclosing any details about Aiden, at least I have my job to brag about.

"Oh, I know. I loved your article in last month's issue," she squeals. I smile proudly because my article last month was fantastic. It was about women trying to do everything, be everything, and how it can lead to feelings of failure when we fall short. I received a great amount of positive feedback. I'm not surprised that Liza enjoyed it— she was some of my inspiration, even though she doesn't know it.

I actually got the idea because not long after baby Knox was born she threw a huge party for my brother's law firm. It was quite the event, and I'm a little surprised she didn't have a breakdown. I think she came close but would never admit it.

Liza and her mother start discussing the article, while I look out into the backyard. I see Kylie and three little girls dressed up in head-to-toe princess gear. Everyone seems to be having a great time. I know I should be embracing this fun family gathering, but I can't help but be distracted. My mind wanders back to Aiden and how perfect last night was. The thought of spending more time with him makes me absolutely giddy.

"Are you excited?" Liza asks.

I give her a funny look. Excited? *Is she a mind reader now?* Can she add that to her lengthy list of great qualities?

"I'm surprised you agreed to it," she continues.

Wait. What is she talking about? I was so busy daydreaming about Aiden that I missed what she said.

"I'm sorry. What did I agree to?" I ask. My stomach begins to twist into a knot as Liza and her mom exchange a glance.

"You don't know? Your mother invited that guy she's trying to set you up with. Is it Wilbur?" she asks cautiously. "I figured you knew because she would never—"

I let out a frustrated sigh and close my eyes. I shouldn't be surprised.

"He goes by Will," I say. "I guess I better go have a chat with my dear mother."

I head out to the deck where Mom is busily talking. She practically jumps off her lounge chair as soon as she sees me. "There's my gorgeous girl," she announces as soon as she sees me.

"Hi, Mom."

She grabs my hand and pulls me over to introduce me to her friends.

"Ladies, this is my Erin. She's the best journalist at *Strike a Pose* magazine," She brushes a few strands of hair off my face. I say hello to her friends and ask if I can talk to her for a minute in private. She follows me back toward the house.

"Is something wrong?" she asks worriedly.

"Mom, did you invite Will to come here today?" I ask her firmly.

She purses her lips and looks away. "I did because he really wants to meet you, and Sharon is a dear friend. Please be nice."

I groan and shake my head. "Mom, I just wanted to enjoy Kylie's party. Why do you have to make it awkward? A first-time meeting at a child's birthday party isn't ideal."

She stares at me as if I'm speaking Chinese.

"You're being silly," she says waving her hand. "It'll be fine. In fact, I think it's a great idea for him to be around the family, so he can get comfortable." Obviously, she hasn't heard a word I've said, or at least, she doesn't care about a word I've said.

"Little sis, when did you get here?" a voice says from behind me. My brother joins my mother and I and puts me in a headlock. Typical. He may be a big shot to all his colleagues, but he's still just an annoying older brother to me. I elbow him in the ribs, and he lets me go.

"A little while ago. I was just talking to Mom about the surprise guest she invited just to meet me." I scowl.

"Oh, that's right," he exclaims. "Mom's using her granddaughter's birthday party to pimp you out." He laughs like it's the funniest thing that's ever happened. Neither Mom nor I find his joke funny.

"Eric, watch your language," she demands. My brother continues to chuckle at his own joke until our father's arrival distracts him. We're actually still getting used to our parents being divorced. They get along so well, you'd never know they weren't together anymore. Eric and Dad give each other a man hug.

"Hi, sweet pie," he says when he sees me.

"Hi, Daddy." I rest my face on his chest and breathe in the familiar scent of Old Spice. He's not even that old, but the man still wears Old Spice.

"Looking good, Margie," he says to my mom as he leans in and gives her a kiss on the cheek.

She beams at his compliment. I shake my head. My parents are so weird. I'm still not exactly sure why they decided to break up. I don't even think they know either.

"Thank you," Mom says sweetly. "Edward, our daughter is mad at me again."

As if it happens a lot. Okay, so maybe it does—but today I have good reason.

"No way?" he says chuckle as he winks at me.

"Yeah, Mom's using this party to pimp Erin out," Eric chimes in. Of course, he starts laughing again. Honestly, it's not funny anymore.

"Eric," my mom reprimands. "I just invited a handsome, successful man to stop by and meet my daughter. Wilbur has really been looking forward to this."

I put my hand to my forehead because I know exactly what's coming.

"Wilbur?" Eric spits out. "You're trying to set Erin up with a guy named Wilbur?" He and my dad look at each other and burst out laughing.

"He goes by Will," I inform them. Of course, they don't hear me over their laughter and tears.

My mom storms off in a huff, and I can't blame her even though I'm still frustrated. "Okay, you guys have made your point."

They manage to stop laughing long enough for Eric to wipe his eyes. "Aw, sis, we're just playing around. I'm sure he's a good guy." He puts his arm around my shoulders. I shove his arm off and head toward where the kids are playing. I'd much rather hang with children who are probably acting more mature than the adults in my family.

Playing with my niece Kylie and her friends is so much better than talking to my mother and brother. She has dragged me back and forth between the bounce house and her playhouse about twenty times. Admittedly, I'll do this all day long if it keeps me away from Eric, my mother, and the men she tries to introduce me to.

As I sit on the grass while the kids race around me, I take a glance around my brother's sprawling backyard. My parents are sitting together on the deck looking awfully cozy, and Mom's holding two-year-old Knox, whose baby giggles are filling the air. I hear my brother announce that the next house tour will begin in two minutes. So far there hasn't been an appearance by Will, and relief begins to wash over me. It's not that I'm completely opposed to meeting him, this just isn't the place I'd want to do it. I'd rather not be the talk of the party, and that's exactly what would happen.

As the party rages on (is that the way to describe a child's party?), I'm actually enjoying myself.

I'm in the middle of a fabulous tea party with Kylie and friends when there's a knock on the playhouse door. Kylie boldly instructs me to answer it.

I glance out to see a cute guy peeking through the window.

"Good-day, do you have room for another guest?"

I'm so caught off guard that I don't know what to say. It doesn't take me long to figure out that this must be the one and only Wilbur.

"Um, sure. Do you like tea?" I ask. He smiles and nods his head. I tell Kylie I'll be back and duck out of the playhouse to introduce myself.

"Erin, right?" he says, flashing me a warm smile.

"You must be Will," I reply. He has wavy brown hair and a square jaw.

"Yes. I'm so sorry about this," he says, waving his arm around. "My mom and Margie have been harassing me nonstop about meeting you. I didn't think today was the right time, but my mother begged me to accompany her, so here I am."

Poor Will, I guess he's also a victim in our mother's diabolical plan. When I look back at the house, I notice my mother is now huddled with a woman I'm assuming is Sharon. They have their heads together as they watch our encounter, obviously proud that their brilliant idea is coming together.

"Well, since you're here, do you want to join us for tea?" I ask.

He chuckles. "I do love a good tea party."

Liza once again proves that she's superwoman. She's thought of every little specific detail to go with the princess theme— the food, the décor, the games. Kylie is in heaven. After Liza brings out a cake that's bigger than Kylie, Will and I have a chance to chat alone while everyone is waiting for a piece.

"Well at least the initial awkwardness is over," Will says with a big grin. "Who knew a tea party could be such a great ice breaker?"

"Yes, the worst is over, except for the fact that we're being watched very closely." I throw a glance to where our mothers are whispering.

"I'll ignore them if you do," he says.

"Deal."

"My mother means well," he adds. "I've tried to tell her that she has nothing to worry about, but her biggest concern in life is that I find someone she gets along with. Of course, that's the most important thing to her. Never mind if I'm interested in them or not."

I laugh. "I don't think my mother cares about that part. She's mostly worried about what her friends think, and somehow my personal life is part of that."

"We could shut them up by meeting up for lunch or something," he suggests.

"You're probably right."

"Great. I'll text you, and we can go from there," he says.

"Sounds good."

Shortly after the big cake presentation, Will and his mother leave. He's actually very nice. Of course I'm not attracted to him like I am to Aiden, but I can definitely see us being friends. They aren't out the door two seconds before my mom pulls me aside to get the scoop.

"Mom, there's nothing to tell," I snap. I can feel my blood pressure rise as she continues to pressure me about giving Will a chance.

"Honey, he's very nice and handsome. Don't rule it out just yet."

"He is, but I'm just not interested right now."

That's definitely not the answer she wants to hear.

"Erin, you have to give it more time. It looked like there was plenty of chemistry from where I was standing."

Of course she does, she only sees what she wants to see, and I don't have the energy to argue with her.

"Did you at least make plans to see each other again?" she continues. She's not going to give up.

"We briefly discussed meeting up for lunch, but that's it."

She still doesn't seem satisfied.

"Mom, we're at your granddaughter's birthday party," I remind her. "I still can't believe you used this day to your advantage."

She shakes her head in frustration. "Oh, don't be so dramatic. I'm only trying to help, and I believe you'll thank me later. Please promise me you'll at least consider meeting with him again."

I finally agree in order to appease her…for now.

My mother and I are the last to leave the party, but not before my brother takes us on a tour of his new soon-to-be man cave.

"Isn't this great?" Eric says proudly.

"Very nice," I say, pretending to act impressed.

I'm mentally exhausted, and I really just want to go home and curl up on my couch.

"Hey, sis, Wilbur seems like a decent guy," Eric says, giving me a smug look. Sometimes I just want to punch my brother. Of course my mom is overjoyed at his comment.

Figures—he always knows exactly what to say to make her happy.

"Mind your own business," I snap. "And since when are you so concerned with my love life?"

He shrugs his shoulders and walks away—typical. It's definitely time for me to go home.

Chapter Five

"*T*ell me every detail." Bre corners me the second I step off the elevator. Surprisingly, she beat me to the office today, which rarely happens. She's definitely pulling out all the stops to be selected for the project.

"Every detail about what?" I ask innocently. Of course, I know exactly what she's talking about. She wants to know about my evening with Aiden, and I'm sure she's curious about Harry, too. She hasn't mentioned him, so I'm assuming he hasn't called her. Maybe he called Aly, although I'm pretty sure she'd tell me right away.

"Don't be daft. You know what I'm talking about," she teases.

I pretend not to hear her. I'm sure it's driving her mad that I'm not spilling all the details.

"Aiden and I had a nice time together," I say shortly. She stares at me as if I've lost my mind.

"A nice time? That's all you have to say?" she asks.

"Yes. Aiden went out of his way to make the evening wonderful."

I remain calm despite remembering the feeling of Aiden's lips on mine for the first time.

"Good morning," Aly announces with a big grin on her face. She's definitely in a very good mood, although I've never seen her in a bad mood. "It's a beautiful day," she adds in a singsong voice. "And...I'm almost finished with the piece I'm submitting for the Bleu Amour. Eek."

This girl belongs in a Disney movie.

I'm beginning to wonder if I'm the only person who isn't ready for this interview.

Bre rolls her eyes. She really isn't very good at hiding her thoughts. I know she doesn't think Aly has a chance in hell of getting one of the spots, but you never know. I really need to get it together. Panic is starting to set in because I'm not satisfied with my article at this point. I've come close to throwing my laptop against the wall a few times. If both Bre and Aly have their work completed, I'm in trouble.

"Good for you," I say trying to cheer her on.

"Thanks, Erin. You've really inspired me," she says, giving me a grateful smile.

That's nice of her to say, but I wish I could say the same for my own inspiration.

But to give myself credit, I've definitely helped Aly more than anyone else has since she started at the magazine.

Bre seems to have lost interest in our conversation and has her back turned toward us. I follow her lead because I have a lot of work to do.

My mind continues to wander as the day goes on. It's been three days since my magical evening with Aiden, and I'm ready for a repeat. Just as I'm about to send him a text, I see him saunter off the elevator. The man has perfect timing.

"Hey, you," he says with a warm smile. And not a mention of the horrific ET nickname.

"I was just about to text you," I say, trying to hold in my excitement.

"Ah, I guess we were thinking about the same thing."

"Aren't you two adorable?" Bre calls from her desk. I'm about to kick the back of her chair when she turns to face us.

"I have a bone to pick with you, Aiden Thomas."

Aiden raises his eyebrows at me. "Oh really, what did I do this time?"

She frowns. "You know what I'm talking about. Have you talked to your brother?"

My stomach twists as I glance at Aly, who's suddenly become very interested in this conversation. Let the fun begin.

"My brother?" Aiden asks. "Why would I want to talk to him?"

I cover my mouth with my hand to keep from laughing. Aly's pretending to be busy, but I know she's intently listening to every word.

"Oh stop," Bre whines.

"Bre, I hate to break it to you, but I have no control over what my brother does," he says with a shrug.

"*Anyway,* the reason I came up here was to invite you to lunch," he says, clearly moving on from the whole Harry-Bre fiasco. "Want to join me?"

That's a silly question.

"I'd love to." I jump to my feet and drag him away. I definitely want to escape just in case a battle over Harry ensues. Poor Aly looked very concerned, so I'm sure she'll have plenty of questions ready for me when I return.

"That was awkward," I say once we are safely on the elevator. "I've been wondering if Harry made a decision yet."

Aiden leans in and gives me a quick, gentle kiss making my legs feel wobbly. He slides away as we stop at another floor on the way down. We move to the side to let the person on the elevator.

"There's no telling what my brother's up too," he continues as if we've been talking the entire time. "I don't know what goes through that guy's mind. He may call one of them or both, or he may run off to Vegas with a random flight attendant. It changes by the day."

I quickly gather my thoughts as I try not to think about our kiss. So, basically he's saying that Harry is a player. Ugh, as much as I want to stay out of this, I should probably warn both Bre and Aly about him. That's what friends are supposed to do...right? But before I warn them, I need more info.

We sit down in the little café right outside our building. "So tell me, is Harry like a huge player or a bum or something? It sounds like he doesn't take anything seriously."

Aiden takes a sip of his water. "Harry is definitely not a *bum*. I would describe him more as free-spirited. To be honest with you, he actually owns a few companies and has become quite successful. Shocking, I know. He acts like he doesn't have a care in the world."

Harry's a CEO? What?

"You're kidding, right?" I ask. There's no way the guy I met is some big business mogul.

He shakes his head. "I'm completely serious. He and a few friends went into business together when they were in college. He didn't graduate college, but the guy makes...let's just say a lot. He owns two homes—a condo here and a beach house on Maui."

"Wow," I say under my breath.

"Oh no. Don't *you* go falling all over him too," he says defensively. "Harry doesn't need another woman chasing him, especially you. And don't say anything to Bre or Aly. He likes to keep that info under wraps, especially in the beginning."

I nod my head. I can understand that.

"Harry thinks people treat him different when they find out." He pauses. "Personally, I think he enjoys being mysterious."

This is fascinating. And it's kind of sweet that Aiden's worried about me falling for Harry's charm.

"Okay, enough about Harry," I say.

"Thank you," he says sounding relieved. "Let's talk about you. How was your niece's birthday party?"

I totally forgot that I mentioned the party while we were on our date.

"It was pretty good, except for my mom and her brilliant ideas," I pause. Do I really want to tell him about her attempts to set me up with Will?

"That sounds interesting. What kind of brilliant ideas?" Aiden asks. *Crap.* Sometimes I don't know when to shut up. Although it shouldn't be a big deal because we've only been out once. We haven't discussed being exclusive with one another, naturally I'm all for it.

I clear my throat. "She invited her friends' son to meet me, and it was awkward considering it was a child's birthday party. My brother spent the afternoon making tasteless jokes about her using the party to pimp me out. Which is pretty typical of him," I say, rolling my eyes.

"Huh…that sounds like something Harry would do. I bet our brothers would get along well."

All of a sudden a coworker from Aiden's department approaches our table.

While he and Aiden chat, it occurs to me that Aiden didn't seem the slightest bit phased or concerned when I mentioned Mom trying to set me up. Maybe he's just trying to play it cool? My phone buzzes, and sure enough it's a text from Will. Wow. I guess timing is everything.

Hey, it's Will. Want to grab dinner this week?

"I'm sorry," Aiden says, pulling me away from the text. "Next time, let's go somewhere away from the office so there's less chance for interruptions."

"Sounds good to me," I reply, putting my phone in my bag. "At least Bre didn't crash our lunch today."

"Definitely."

Thankfully there's no more mention about the birthday party or my mother's meddling in my life.

When I return to the office, Bre is gone. She's probably taking one of her usual extended lunches. In other words, she'll surface in a few hours. Aly's still at her desk, scrolling through her phone.

"How was your lunch?" she asks when she sees me.

"Good," I reply, a broad smile spreading across my face.

"You and Aiden make a great couple," she says.

I can feel my cheeks turning red. Which is silly because it's not like my interest in Aiden has ever been a secret, and why should I care what anyone thinks anyway?

"Can I ask you something?" she says twisting a piece of her blonde hair around her finger.

I think I already know what this is about.

"Is something going on between Bre and Harry?" Ah, I knew it was coming. And I'm going to be honest with her.

"I don't think anything's happened, but she expressed interest after we all met him."

I'm not really sure what else to say.

"I totally get it," she exclaims after a few seconds. "You've known Bre longer than me, so of course you'd want your boyfriend's brother to date her."

Whoa. Where did this surprise outburst come from? I'm speechless because, first of all, I couldn't really care less who Harry dates, and second, Aiden isn't exactly my boyfriend —yet.

"That's not true," I say calmly. Yes, I've known Bre longer, but whom Harry chooses to date or not has nothing to do with me.

"It doesn't really matter anyway," she says with a shrug. "Everything works out the way it's supposed to in the end." She turns back to her desk, leaving me feeling confused. I haven't seen this side of Aly before. All of a sudden she seems sure of herself, almost overly confident, and she was a little short with me.

"Aly, I can assure you I have nothing to do with Harry Thomas's personal life, and neither does Aiden," I remind her. I'm not sure why I feel the need to give her any kind of explanation.

"I know," she says finally. "Sorry if I was rude. You've been so helpful to me since I got here."

Our conversation is interrupted by Bre's return. Aly scowls and turns back to her desk. Ugh, I really need to get my own office and the sooner the better.

∼

This is the absolute best time to be in the office. It's six o'clock, and almost everyone has gone home for the day. I'm still trying to work on my article, and I've changed the topic more times than I can count. I had to take a break and work on my submission for this month—just in time to make my deadline. The theme is tips and ideas for travelers. I've spent months researching best times to book air travel, top-tier hotels, and other vacation tips. People can't get enough travel articles, so that's my safe and happy place. I considered using it for my interview piece, but I just don't think it's good enough. It has to be something that captures the interview panel. The clock is ticking, and interviews should be starting next week. Chelsie said the team will be heading to Paris within the next two months.

Just as I'm about to throw my computer across the room yet again, I realize that I need a break. When I check my phone, I remember that I never responded to Will's text about getting together. In my defense I was with Aiden, so I was preoccupied.

I let out a deep sigh. There's no reason I can't go out with Will *as friends*. Aiden and I haven't discussed being exclusive and meeting up with Will would get my mother off my case, which would be a definite plus. I finally respond to his text.

Sure. Sounds good.

As soon as I finish texting Will, my phone rings.

"Hello."

"I was getting ready to file a missing person's report. Where have you been?" Mia exclaims. She's yelling so loudly I have to pull the phone away from my ear.

A feeling of guilt washes over me. Sometimes I get so caught up in my life that I don't talk to my best friend for weeks at a time. Mia and I have been best friends since we were teenagers. She lives in Florida now, but we try to see each other at least once a year if possible.

"I know," I reply. "There's a lot happening at work, and you know me when it comes to my job."

Mia knows me better than anyone in this world, probably even better than I know myself. It was a hard transition when she moved to Florida. Truthfully, I'm really not good at making new friends. Some people may even say I'm antisocial, especially on those nights I'd rather be at home watching TV than going to happy hour.

"Girl, I really think you need a vacation," she exclaims. "How about a trip to Miami to see your fabulous best friend?"

I smile to myself. "Speaking of traveling, I'm interviewing for a two-month project, and the location is pretty spectacular." I feel like there should be a drum roll playing in the background.

"Oh, really? Where might this location be, and can you bring a guest?"

I giggle. I knew she was going to ask about coming with me.

"It's just Paris," I say nonchalantly.

"Okay, when do we leave," she asks after a few seconds of silence.

"Very funny. I don't have the job yet."

"No, but I'm sure you'll get it. Star journalist Erin Taylor is the best that *Strike a Pose* has," she says confidently.

I wish I had her faith in me.

"Well, there's a lot of competition and only a few spots. I'm still trying to decide what I want to write about while my coworkers are locked and loaded with their submissions," I wail.

"Erin, you got this. Don't stress."

Ha. Easy for her to say.

"In other news, I have to tell you about my evening with Aiden."

This is the perfect topic to draw her attention away from Paris. She's completely silent as I give her all the wonderful details of my dream date.

"He even had a blanket ready for when I got cold," I exclaim.

"Ooohhhh," she breathes. "I love the attention to detail. Very impressive."

This isn't our first conversation about Aiden, considering I've had a crush on him for quite a while. Mia's spent many phone calls listening to me ramble on about him.

"It all sounds so dreamy," she says. "You know, you could bring Aiden with you to Miami. I bet he and Jack would get along great."

Jack is Mia's boyfriend, whom I've never met in person. I think he may be a long-lost Hemsworth brother because he's just as hot as Liam...or Chris...well, one of them. Most importantly, he treats my best friend like a queen. You can't get much better than that.

"Slow your roll. It's only been one date. We're hardly to the point of planning vacations together."

Mia laughs. "Why not?"

I scoff. "On another note, my mother has reached a new level of nightmare."

"No way. Not Margie," she says pretending to sound shocked.

I give her the scoop about my mom inviting Will to Kylie's party. Mia is very familiar with my complicated relationship with my mother.

"So, do you have a picture of Will?" she asks. "Is he at least good-looking? Is he your type, or did Margie just pick him because he has a pulse?"

I laugh. Here I am giving her the details of my latest public humiliation, and she's more curious about what Will looks like. "He's attractive."

Of course he's not a long-lost Hemsworth brother who sells yachts to rich people in Miami, but I don't say this out loud. "You can look up his profile online."

She doesn't say anything which means she's already on it.

"Ohhh, he is cute," she squeals.

"He is. And I did finally agree to meet up with him," I tell her. "If that's what it takes to get Margie to chill, it's worth it."

"Definitely," she agrees.

Somehow I manage to get her off the phone with a promise to keep her updated on the Paris trip. Between Aiden, Will, my mother and my coworkers, it'll be a miracle if I'm able to focus on the task at hand.

∾

"Honestly, I need a new cubicle, or I'd be more than happy to take one of those tiny offices that no one is using."

It's my monthly meeting with Chelsie, and I'm pleading my case about moving my desk.

"I know it sounds silly, but I don't think I'm reaching my full potential right now."

"Because of where you sit," Chelsie says trying to hide her smile.

She probably thinks I'm losing it—and maybe I am. I'm trying especially hard not to throw the other girls under the bus, but I may get desperate.

"Erin, I can't just give you an office," she says pushing her glasses up on the bridge of her nose. "What's going on with you lately?"

I'm not sure how much I want to tell her. Telling your boss that you're struggling with creativity and writer's block probably isn't the best idea.

I've worked with Cheslie for a while, and she knows how dedicated I am to my work. It doesn't surprise me that she can sense my distress. I have to get creative. I don't want to tell her that I can't concentrate on my job because I'm distracted by my coworkers' potential love triangle. Or that my mother is meddling in my personal life.

"Is it that obvious?" I ask her. "Just some drama with my mother, and of course, the pressure is on for the Paris job."

Chelsie leans back in her chair and places her pen cap to her lips.

"Erin, I seriously doubt you have anything to worry about. I truly believe you have a good shot at one of those positions. Your dedication to your work far exceeds anyone else's on our team. Of course, I'm not making the final decision, but I have complete faith in you."

I appreciate her positivity, and it does calm my nerves a bit. I'm about to leave her office when I remember what Aiden said about other opportunities here. Now would be a good time to get Chelsie's thoughts.

"Can I ask you one more thing?" I say, sitting back down across from her desk.

"Always," she says, giving me a curious look.

I shift around in my chair. "Let's say I don't get chosen for the project. Any chance there would be more opportunities for those who stay here?"

"What do you mean?" she asks, raising her eyebrows. "Don't you want to go? I thought everyone in this building would be fighting tooth and nail to get there."

Of course, I'd love the chance to work in Paris for two months, but then what? When the project is over, I'll most likely be back here and stuck dealing with Bre and Aly day in and day out.

"I'd absolutely love to go. I was just thinking long term." I trail off because I can tell Chelsie's processing what I'm saying. At least, I think she is. For all I know she could be thinking about *Bridgerton*. There have to be other people with a TV addiction like mine. Right?

"We can discuss that after the interview process is done," she says finally. "But, in the meantime, you shouldn't worry too much about it."

I leave her office feeling hopeful. I guess I should feel good that Chelsie has so much confidence in my abilities.

When I return to my desk, I find Aiden waiting for me. I instantly feel better. He's sitting comfortably in my chair, talking to Aly.

"Thank you so much, Aiden," she says. "It's really hard being the new girl, and I want to do everything I can to prove myself. This would be a huge start to my career, and it helps knowing someone on the interview panel." She reaches over and puts her hand on his knee.

Whoa, what the hell?

A massive wave of jealousy washes over me.

"This is a nice surprise," I say loudly, letting them know I've returned.

"There you are," he says, his face lighting up. Aly looks over at me and smiles but doesn't move her hand.

Hmm...I could always remove it for her.

"Aiden and I were just chatting about the interviews," she exclaims while slowly pulling away from him.

"I told him how much I appreciate your encouragement."

I give a nod.

"Of course," I say calmly.

Aiden gets up from my chair. "I need to get back, but I just wanted to come say hi."

Damn. He's already leaving.

"I'm sorry. My meeting with Chelsie went a little long," I say with a frown. Aly is still watching us. I shoot her a glance, but she doesn't take my hint.

"I'll walk with you," I say, linking my arm in his.

"I'd like that," he says. "See you later, Aly.

When we are safely inside the elevator, I immediately bring up Aly.

"Did she ask you about Harry again? She knows Bre's interested in him too."

He shakes his head. "Surprisingly, no. She was asking a lot about the interview process. She must think I have more influence on the decision than I really do."

The elevator quickly arrives at his floor. "Anyway, I wanted to make plans for dinner, but I have to jump on a call. Can we talk later?"

I smile. "Of course."

"Awesome." He leans in and kisses me on the cheek.

I'm in a complete daze as the elevator sails back to my floor. Maybe I overreacted to seeing Aly's hand on Aiden's knee. He didn't seem a bit phased by it, so I probably shouldn't be either. Aly is busily typing when I return, which is exactly what I need to be doing.

Chapter Six

"*E*rin, I don't understand why you haven't made the time to go out with Wilbur yet."

"Will," I remind her.

I'm on my weekly call with my mother, and of course she doesn't ask how I'm doing or about my job or anything else. Nope, all she cares about is Will and me.

"Mom, I've been busy. We have a lot going on at the magazine," I explain. And in my defense, Will must be busy too because I haven't heard back from him since I agreed to go to dinner.

"Well, Sharon and I had brunch a few days ago, and we're both eager for you two to spend some time together," she replies. "We agree that you and Wilbur are a perfect match."

"And how would you know?" I exclaim. I'm trying to keep my cool, but she makes it nearly impossible.

"Oh, trust me, you'll understand when you're a mother."

I let out an exasperated sigh. That's her go-to answer anytime I question her ideas.

"Even your father agrees. He really liked Will."

Now's my chance to flip this around and put her in the hot seat. "What's going on with you and Dad? You sure spend a lot of time together for two people who just got divorced."

My question must've caught her off guard because she doesn't say anything for a few seconds.

"I'm not sure what you mean," she says defensively.

"I guess I'm just confused as to why you got divorced in the first place. You two seemed pretty close at the party."

"Erin, we were married a long time, we have a family together, and we're best friends. There's nothing wrong with our relationship," she insists. "And you shouldn't be so worried about my love life and worry about your own."

Ouch, that was harsh.

"Okay, I need to go, Mom. I'll keep you posted on things." I hang up quickly.

About an hour after I get off the phone with my mother, I get a text from Will.

Sharon and Margie are relentless. Let's go to dinner

I laugh out loud. I guess he had a similar conversation with Sharon as I did with my mother. I send him a response.

I agree.

We text back and forth for a while, making plans for Saturday. I consider calling my mom back to tell her that Will and I have made plans but decide to let her suffer for a few days instead.

After Will and I finalize everything, I get back to working on my submission, and I finally finish. At least, I think I finished. I even resist the urge to turn on the TV. I'm definitely feeling more confident than I was a few days ago, and I think my meeting with Chelsie helped. Now that my article is done, I should be able to sleep better. And hopefully Aiden and I will be making plans for another magical evening together. Things are definitely starting to look up.

This morning I woke up feeling like I can conquer the world. As soon as I step off the elevator, my morning gets even better when I see Aiden leaning against my desk. Although he's talking to Aly…again. I know it shouldn't bother me because he's here waiting for me (at least, I think he is).

"Good morning," I say cheerfully. I refuse to show how irritated I am.

"Hey," Aiden says. "I was hoping to catch you this morning. How are you?"

Ah-ha, so he is waiting for me.

"I'm great," I say excitedly. "I finally finished my article late last night."

"Fantastic," Aly chimes in.

I purposely ignore her. I know it's not her fault that Aiden keeps showing up looking for me, but there are some things that aren't acceptable. Her hand on his knee was totally against girl code.

"Good for you," he says, putting his arm around me as he pulls me in for a side hug. A side hug—I guess it's better than nothing at this point, and we are in the office. I certainly can't expect him to pull me into a full embrace right here in front of everyone.

"Does that mean you have a few minutes to grab coffee with me?" he asks.

Ha. Like he has to ask.

"I would love that," I say. Aly remains quiet. This is a good reminder for her that Aiden is here to see me.

I take my laptop out of my bag and leave it on my desk. I'm practically floating as Aiden and I walk around the block to the coffee shop, chatting the entire time about work. Once we're away from the office, Aiden puts his arm around me and kisses me on the forehead. I take advantage of this moment and wrap my arms around his waist.

"I've missed you," he whispers.

My heart pounds, and all thoughts of work, Paris, and Aly disappear from my mind.

"I'm glad to hear it," I say with coy smile.

He raises an eyebrow. "That's it? I was expecting an 'I've missed you, too.'"

"Okay, maybe I've missed you a little," I tease.

After we get our coffee, we sit down at an outdoor table. It's a beautiful, sunny day with a light breeze. Aiden leans toward me and puts his hand on my leg.

"So ET, how about dinner on Saturday night?"

How does he expect me to keep my composure when he touches me?

"Saturday would be perfect," I say softly. He moves his chair closer to mine and leans in to kiss me but then stops and pulls back.

He cringes. "I probably shouldn't kiss you while we're on the clock."

I frown. "Yeah, I guess not."

"I want to," he whispers, sending tingles up and down my spine.

Ugh. This is torture. *Why do we have to be at work? Is it too late to call in sick?*

We chat for a few minutes before heading back to the office with our coffees.

Thankfully we're the only two on the elevator as we sail up to our floors, so Aiden leans in and kisses me on the cheek before getting off. As soon as the door closes, I do a little dance of excitement. I'm practically floating back to my desk, trying to tone down my smile. Bre has arrived because her stuff is thrown all over her desk.

"How was your coffee meeting?" Aly asks as soon as she seems me.

"Just fine," I say, setting my cup down on the desk. "Did Aiden say anything about Harry while he was here?" I ask. I certainly wasn't going to use my time with Aiden to talk about his brother. I'm actually surprised that Aly hasn't brought him up at all.

"Nah, I figured that he would've reached out to me by now if he was interested," she says with a shrug. "Aiden is really great though."

"Mm-hmm," I say, trying to ignore the nagging vibe I'm getting from her.

"He's so encouraging. You guys definitely have that in common," she continues.

The more she talks about Aiden the more it bothers me. I've never considered myself a jealous person. And Aiden can talk to anyone he wants. I'm the one who's having dinner with another man.

Wait. *Oh no!* I'm supposed to have dinner with Will on Saturday night, but I just told Aiden I could go out with him the same night.

"Crap, what did I do?" I exclaim out loud, interrupting Aly's rambling. She gives me a strange look.

"What's wrong?"

"Oh," I pause. "I just realized I forgot about something and double-booked myself." I dig for my phone as I try to figure out how to get myself out of this mess. Of course I want to go out with Aiden again, but my mom will lose it if she finds out I made plans and then canceled on Will.

"Where were you?" Bre asks, rushing off the elevator. "I have a crisis, and I need to talk to you now."

Ugh. Now is not the time for one of her crises, especially when I'm having my own crisis.

"Give me a second," I plead. I scroll through my phone, looking for Will's number.

All of a sudden my desk phone rings. Ugh. Why does everything happen all at once?

"This is Erin," I answer.

"Hey, it's Chelsie. Can you come to my office really quick?"

Now?

"Uh sure."

I want to scream. My day was off to such a great start. The relief of finishing my article and coffee with Aiden are quickly becoming overshadowed. I was so excited to make plans that I totally forgot about dinner with Will.

I'm still scrolling through my phone. *What am I looking for?* I'm so frazzled.

"Erin, this is really important," Bre wails.

I find Will's number and send him a quick text.

Something came up on Saturday. Does Friday work?

"I'll be back. Chelsie needs me." I put my phone down on the desk and head to her office.

As soon as I sit down, Chelsie starts asking me about my next few submissions. *Why does she have to do this now?*

"Of course, if you're in Paris, we'll find someone else to cover your article."

Ugh. What if I don't want someone else to cover it? This is the one aspect of working abroad that bothers me. I need to remember to look at the big picture. My future is here, and if I want to advance in my career, I need to show everyone that I can handle anything.

"No, I can still do it," I insist. "I can start now and have them ready to submit while I'm gone." I pause. "I mean, *if* I'm gone.

I'm probably getting a head of myself. I haven't interviewed yet.

Chelsie smiles. "I expected you to say that. Why don't we revisit this after the interviews? An official announcement will be released sometime today."

Here we go, I think to myself. It'll be mass hysteria by the end of the day.

"Wow, it's getting real," I say, exhaling.

"Yes, it is," she says. "Things are about to go into overdrive around here."

"I was just thinking the same thing."

I feel a sense of relief that I already have my piece done for my interview. I head back to my desk to find Bre with an ice pack on her head. Really? That's a bit overdramatic even for Bre. Aly is busily typing on her laptop.

"There you are. I need you," Bre wails. "Take a walk with me."

She grabs my arm and drags me toward the conference room. Ugh. I haven't even had a chance to sit down at my desk yet.

"I have a huge dilemma," she says as she shuts and locks the door.

"I had a feeling—I think the ice pack was a good indication," I say, with a giggle.

"Never mind this," she says, throwing the ice on the table. "I met with the dating doctor a few days ago. Following our meeting, he put me in contact with two fantastic men." She stops and inhales deeply. "Come to find out they're cousins and both really great. And then to complicate my life further, your stupid boyfriend's brother finally calls me."

She pauses and lets out a heavy sigh. "Seriously, it's too much stress for one person to handle. And I'm going to be in Paris soon, so it's probably not the best time to start a new relationship."

My head is spinning right now. This was her huge crisis? Of course she thinks she's going to Paris. That's classic, Bre.

"Okay, just calm down a second. Maybe you're getting ahead of yourself."

She gives me a questioning look.

"Why don't you get to know these men before you make up your mind?"

"I guess," she says with a shrug. "Can you talk to Aiden and get the story on Harry? He seems so elusive, but I know there's more to him than meets the eye."

It's not my place to tell her what I know about Harry.

"What makes you say that?" I ask.

"I have to tell you something," she says in a low whisper. "I did some research, and Harry is actually Harrison Thomas. Supposedly he buys and sells companies. I don't know all the details, but I'm very interested to learn all there is to know about the man."

This is the Bre I know. Aiden is naïve to think that she wouldn't do her homework.

"Well, what did Harry say when he called?" I ask. I'm actually pretty curious to hear how the conversation went. I didn't want to be involved—but it's too late now.

"He asked me out to a Warrior's game. I'm not really into basketball, but I certainly wasn't going to tell him that, and he has seats on the floor. I would've been crazy to turn those down. I'm just curious if Harry said anything to Aiden about me. I would ask him myself, but I already know he's not going to tell me anything. Your man can be super annoying sometimes."

I roll my eyes.

"He's not my man," I say, trying to hide my smile.

She waves her hand. "Yeah, sure."

"Will you ask him for me?" she begs. She seems more relaxed now, nothing like the girl who rushed in here with an ice pack on her head.

"What makes you think he'll tell me anything?" I ask.

She gives me a wicked smile. "I'm sure you could find a way to convince him."

Um, no. There's no way I'm stooping to those levels to get information about Aiden's brother. There are so many things wrong with that idea.

"I'm going to ignore that comment and go back to my desk. I haven't done a thing all day." I start to head for the door when she links her arm in mine.

"What's the deal with your new best friend, Aly? You two have certainly become close," she suggests.

"Why don't you like Aly?" I ask.

She shrugs her shoulders. "There's just something about her, and you should probably watch your back. I don't think she's as sweet as she acts. You already got her hopes up—the poor girl thinks she has a chance of going to Paris. She's worked at this magazine all of five minutes."

Ha, pot meet the kettle. Bre's also overly confident that she's going to Paris. She'll probably lose her mind if Aly gets chosen and she doesn't.

"We don't know who's going to be selected," I remind her. "And she could very well be one of them. She did get a job at the same magazine as us."

Bre gives a nonchalant shrug. "We'll see."

"Can we go back to work now?" I ask, opening the door.

"Fine," she says, exhaling loudly.

"Erin, your phone has been blowing up," Aly exclaims when Bre and I return from the conference room. She eyes us curiously. When I look at my phone, I see I have six text messages and two missed calls. A few of the messages are from Will about rescheduling and saying Friday night works. I'm about to text him back when a call comes in from my mother. Does she know I changed plans on Will? Maybe he told his mom and then she told mine. Ugh. This is just too much.

I let her call go to voice mail. I can't spend any more of my day dealing with nonsense.

"You're very popular today," Aly suggests. She's staring at me, which causes a strange feeling to wash over me. *Did she look at my phone? Maybe she saw the texts from Will? Wait—would she actually snoop through my phone?*

Bre's comment about watching my back comes to my mind.

"I guess," I say nonchalantly.

"Mm-hmm."

Ugh, I can't let Bre's stupid conspiracy theory get into my head. I have no reason to believe that Aly has some ulterior motive.

I try to push it out of my head and check my emails for the first time today. As expected, a message from Chelsie hits my inbox.

All interviews for the Paris location project will begin on Tuesday. If you haven't done so yet, please respond at your earliest convenience with your submission. These will be reviewed over the next few days by Madeline Bufont and team, and those moving forward will be scheduled for an interview. Serious submissions only. Make Strike a Pose *proud.*

Here we go, game on. I need to make a few more tweaks to my article, and then I can send it over.

"Erin, did you see the email?" Aly calls. "I just sent over my submission. I'm so nervous."

I hear Bre snort. Why does she need to be so rude?

Aly must notice and makes a face. "What about you, Bre? Did you submit yet?"

Bre looks up from her phone. "Of course. I've been doing this a long time, unlike some people."

Ouch. Awkward. Although I suppose this is how it will be moving forward. We're all battling it out for the same four positions.

"Erin, you're probably feeling pretty good right now. You have the best chance out of all of us at one of those spots," Aly adds.

What's that supposed to mean? Bre looks over and gives me a puzzled look.

"I have no better chance than anyone else." I say defensively.

"Sure you do," she replies. "Aiden is on the interview committee, and you're dating him. That's a huge leg up."

Bre raises her eyebrows.

I shoot a glare at Aly. Really? What is she trying to do?

"I didn't mean anything by that," Aly says, backpedaling. "I was just thinking that it must be nice to have a friendly face on the panel."

It's too late. She already made the comment.

"There's a whole panel making the decision, not just one person," I remind her.

Bre goes back to her phone without another word.

I can't get caught up in all of this drama. The only thing I should be focusing on is sending in my own article.

When I open my laptop, I immediately notice something's wrong. My document is open and about a quarter of it is missing. My heart starts to sink into the pit of my stomach. What happened to my ending? Panic begins to set in. Did I not save the final copy? I was up so late working, maybe I didn't save it. I'm going to cry. I frantically search through my recent documents, and sure enough, my completed article is nowhere to be found.

"No, no, no," I exclaim.

What's wrong?" Bre asks.

"Do you still have that ice pack? I may need it."

Stay calm, Erin. I put my forehead in my hands. This is totally okay. I can come back from this—and it will be better than it was.

What a mess. I have edited and changed my article about four times, and it's still not right. I can't seem to wrap it up like it was. When everyone leaves the office for the day, I'm finally able to concentrate.

I can't believe I did this. Am I so overwhelmed that I'm being careless? I've never lost a document, especially something this important.

How did I get to this point? My day started out so fantastic. Somehow over the last few hours, I've managed to lose the perfect ending to my very important article, I've made plans with Will for Friday and with Aiden for Saturday. This is out of character for me. I'm certainly not one to juggle different men. Even though I'm going out with Will to keep my mother off my back. I would say that's a legitimate reason.

I take a few seconds to respond to Will's text about dinner on Friday.

And to top it all off, I can't shake the feeling that Aly is up to something. I'm starting to wonder if she looked at my phone while I was dealing with Bre's issues. If she did, then she obviously saw the texts from Will. It's not like I have anything to hide anyway. When I mentioned it to Aiden, he didn't seem a bit phased by it, and we haven't talked about being exclusive. I don't owe anyone an explanation, but what if she says something to Aiden?

Here I go again, worrying about my personal life. These distractions are going to interfere with my career. Okay, so maybe that's a bit dramatic, but still, I need to focus.

I'm suddenly startled by a noise. That's strange—I thought everyone was gone. I grab a stapler, because a stapler is a perfect way to defend myself should I need it. My heart begins to race when I hear someone come around the corner.

It's Bre. We both scream when we see each other.

"What the hell, Bre? I almost hit you with this." I fall back into my chair.

"You almost hit me with your stapler?" she exclaims. "Savage."

Why is Bre here after work hours? She's rarely here *during* work hours. This is weird. In fact, this whole day has been weird.

"What are you doing here?" I ask her.

She opens her mouth but doesn't say anything. Clearly, she's up to something.

"I just forgot to take care of a few things." She sits down at her desk and opens her laptop.

I turn my chair to face her and silently wait for her to notice.

She looks over at me. "What?"

She's obviously forgotten that I've worked with her for years. I know she'd never be at the office this late. Maybe she is taking this new opportunity seriously.

"Nothing. I'm just surprised to see you," I say.

She frowns. "Why? I work here, too."

Does she really want me to get into this with her? Her defensiveness makes me more suspicious of her.

"So, are you here this late every day? I know you live for this place, but there's more to life than work," she asks.

I want to give her a snarky reply but resist the urge.

"Not usually, I had an issue with my article, so I figured I'd take advantage of the quiet." I reread the same sentence for the third time and change a few more words. I really don't need the distraction of her being here.

"What happened?" she asks curiously.

I let out a heavy sigh before telling her about the missing part of my article.

"Hold on," she says, leaning back in her chair. "You, Erin Taylor—star employee—deleted one of the most important articles of your career. It's not possible."

What's that supposed to mean? I've never thought of myself as a "star employee."

"It *is* possible. I'm just not sure how it happened. I certainly didn't mean to do it." I take a sip of my water. I really wish it was wine after the day I've had.

"It just seems strange," she exclaims. "You're so organized and on top of everything."

I sigh. "Yeah, well, sometimes things just happen."

"Anyway, how late are you planning on staying?" she asks. "You really need to give yourself a break once in a while."

"Not until I'm finished," I insist.

She rolls her eyes and starts typing on her laptop.

Thankfully she allows me to work in peace which is more than she does during normal business hours.

Bre leaves before me, and I'm still confused as to why she was here after hours. Maybe she's starting to take her job seriously. Stranger things have happened.

Chapter Seven

I really don't want to go out with Will tonight. It's been one of the longest weeks ever, and I'm pretty sure that a night curled up in front of the TV is really what I need.

After hours of writing, editing, and some crying, I finally sent in my submission, so now I just wait to find out if I get a callback for an interview.

Meanwhile, Aly is walking around the office like she owns the place. She's become a completely different person from when she first started. A few of my coworkers have made comments about it, and I've noticed that she's gone out of her way to be Chelsie's new bestie. I want to remind her that she's not going to get very far considering Chelsie has nothing to do with the interviews. Although she's made it pretty clear that she doesn't need my help anymore, and I'm glad.

So here I am, getting ready for an evening that I want no part of. Tomorrow night with Aiden will feel completely different.

And thankfully there's no mention of a double with his brother and Bre. Although seeing Bre in action might be quite entertaining.

As soon as I'm ready, I walk to the window to see if I spot Will. There's no sign of him yet, so I look out over the view that I love so much. The brilliant city lights are exhilarating, and I've always loved how the bay glistens below them. I really think San Francisco is one of the grandest cities in the world. Granted, I've never been to Paris, at least not yet, but my heart belongs to San Fran. When I found this apartment, I knew I had to live here no matter how rent poor I'd be.

A knock on the door snaps me from my daydream—that must be Will. I take a deep breath and head to the door.

My stomach is killing me, and not because I'm sick. Will is absolutely hysterical. I can't remember the last time I laughed so hard. As soon as he picked me up, he started our evening by making jokes about inviting our mothers to join us for dinner. By the time we arrive at the restaurant, I totally forget that I didn't want to go out with him.

"Let's go ahead and get the awkward stuff out of the way," he says, taking a piece of bread out of the basket. "Ladies first. Tell me everything about Erin Taylor."

I make a face. "Are you sure?"

He folds his arms in front of himself and leans on the table.

"Okay, I was born here in the Bay Area. As you know, I have one obnoxious brother and a delightful mother. I graduated from Pepperdine with a degree in journalism. I've been at *Strike a Pose* for two years. I love hamburgers, and I have a horrible TV addiction. That's it. I'm incredibly boring."

When I finish, he's pretending to doze off.

"Very funny," I say, banging on the table. "Your turn."

"Hmm...okay, my family is originally from Southern California. I grew up near La Jolla. I have three sisters, and my mom is also delightful. I studied pre-law at UCLA but then changed my major because I realized how much I hated law. So now I run an office equipment company, and I'm thinking about legally changing my name from Wilbur to Will."

We both laugh, and I tell him about how Eric was teasing me about his name at the birthday party. Will has a great attitude, and I love that he can laugh at himself.

After dinner, we head down to Pier 39. I hardly ever come down here. It's nice just to enjoy the sights of our awesome city. I'm having a great time, except that as the night goes on, I'm starting to feel guilty. I'm having such a strong attack of conscience, so I decide to spill the beans.

"I have to tell you something," I blurt out.

He gives me a curious look. "Okay, but why do you suddenly sound so serious? You're freaking me out."

I don't want to put a damper on the evening, but I feel like I should tell him about Aiden.

"I just want to be honest," I say.

He nods his head. "Go for it."

I tell him about Aiden and our date tomorrow night. He doesn't say anything for a few seconds.

"Are you kidding? Why would you go out with me tonight and then go out with another man tomorrow night?" He asks, his tone serious.

Whoa. I wasn't expecting that kind of reaction. I thought this night was to appease our mother's incessant nagging about us getting together. It certainly wasn't my intention to hurt his feelings.

I'm just about to apologize when he cracks a smile and then starts laughing. I'm speechless. *Seriously?* I was just about to grovel for forgiveness because I thought he was genuinely upset.

"You're mean," I say, playfully punching him on the arm. "I was being honest, while you were giving me a pretend guilt trip."

"I'm sorry," he says, trying to hide a smile. "And I should be honest with you too. I'm seeing someone else. We've only been out a few times, so far."

"Well, my mother is going to be heartbroken," I tell him.

"So is mine," he agrees. "That being said, we should hang out again sometime. As friends, of course."

"That would be fun," I say.

"Okay, just to be clear, we're officially friend-zoning each other?" he asks.

I laugh. Will has a great sense of humor.

"Yes."

"Works for me," he says with a shrug.

When I get home, I change into my pajamas and lay on the couch, covering myself with a large fluffy blanket. I had a lot of fun with Will, and at some point I should thank my mother for introducing me to a new friend.

~

"What do you mean you'll be great friends?" my mother wails.

She didn't waste any time to call and get the details of my evening with Will. Forget sleeping in—she wasn't going to give up until I answered.

"We mutually agreed that we'd be friends. I'm sorry to disappoint you."

This conversation is absolutely futile because we rarely see eye to eye on things—my personal life being one of them.

"Erin, sometimes these things take time. You should go out again, get to know each other better, and see if you're compatible."

I sigh. I know she means well, but it's still exhausting.

"We talked about hanging out again—as friends. But if it's any consolation, I'm glad you introduced us."

She's quiet for a few seconds. "That's not a consolation in the slightest. Erin, I'm very worried about you. You need to get out more," she says softly.

I think back to my many nights in front of the TV. She might have a point.

"Although, now that I think about it, most of the greatest love stories begin with friendship." She continues, "Perhaps this is all happening the way it's supposed to."

I glance at the clock. I could stop this nonsense if I tell her about Aiden, but that would open a whole Q and A session I'm not ready for this early in the morning.

"You know your father and I started as friends, and look how wonderful things turned out for us."

What is she talking about? They just woke up one day and decided to get a divorce. I'm about to remind her of this important little fact, but I've probably disappointed her enough for one day.

"Mom, I promise that you have nothing to worry about," I assure her. "My main focus right now is my career. We have some big opportunities coming up soon."

I owe her some good news after shattering her heart.

"In fact, I just submitted an article that's being reviewed for a two-month project overseas." I'm waiting on the edge of my seat to see if she shows any enthusiasm for this job.

"Okay."

"Aren't you the slightest bit curious as to where the project is?"

"Where?" she asks flatly.

Not exactly the reaction I was expecting, but okay.

"It's at our sister magazine in Paris," I exclaim. "Of course, I haven't gotten the job yet, but I think I have a really good chance."

Once the news of Paris registers, she becomes more interested and even suggests that she should come visit me while I'm there. The thought of my mother crashing my trip makes my palms sweat. I hurry off the phone before I make the mistake of telling her what I really think of her joining me in Paris.

I'm just about to get into the shower, when I get a phone call from Aiden. He tells me he thinks he has food poisoning and has to cancel our date. I try to pretend to not be disappointed, and of course little doubts are creeping in making me wonder if he's really sick. *Why am I so quick to jump to that conclusion?*

"I'm so sorry. Can I bring you something?" I ask.

"Um, I'd rather you not see me like this—I've barely been able to leave the bathroom."

"Got it," I say with a cringe.

Sigh. It looks like a long night of watching TV is ahead of me.

"I promise I'll make it up to you," he adds.

"I'll hold you to it." I say, feeling my face get hot.

He abruptly gets off the phone, and I assume the bathroom is calling.

I try to force all negative thoughts out of my mind. Everyone gets sick—unfortunately the timing couldn't be worse.

As soon as I get off the phone with Aiden, I call Mia. I could use a good pep talk from my best friend.

"I want to hear about your evening with Will," she says. "Is Mama Margie ordering the wedding invitations?"

I roll my eyes.

"She wishes," I say, taking a pint of ice cream out of my freezer. "But I actually had a lot of fun."

I grab a spoon. Junk food is totally acceptable when your date cancels. I really think they should put it on the label. I might write a letter and make this suggestion.

"It turns out that Will's also been seeing someone else," I tell her. "He went out with me to appease his mother too."

"Do you want me to call Margie and tell her to get off your back? She might listen to me."

This is true. Mia might be one of the only people who could talk some sense into her.

"Probably, but I won't put you through that. Plus, I haven't told her about Aiden yet either. I know she just thinks I'm hopeless when it comes to relationships and my life consists of sitting home on Saturday nights eating ice cream and watching TV."

I glance down at my half-eaten pint of Cherry Garcia. *Well...crap.*

"What's happening with Aiden anyway?" she asks. "Are you bringing him to Florida to meet me yet?"

I wish. It would be amazing to take a trip with Aiden. I can see us riding rides at Disney World together. Walking through the park, holding hands under the fireworks. Ahhh...

"Hello?" Mia exclaims.

I totally zoned out envisioning a fabulous Florida vacation with my dream man.

"Sorry, I'm here," I say finally. "You'll be the first to know when and if we are ready to plan a trip together."

"It's only a matter of time," she says knowingly.

"I'm supposed to be with him right now, but he's spending his Saturday night on the toilet thanks to food poisoning."

"Ew. Too much information," she wails.

I tell her about how I'm wallowing alone in my apartment due to the last-minute cancellation.

"Don't overthink it," she insists. "He told you he'll make it up to you."

She's absolutely right. I just needed to hear it from someone else.

A few hours later I'm about to crawl into bed when a text comes through from Aiden.

I'm so sorry I had to cancel. I really wish I could've seen you tonight.

It's funny how a simple text can make all my doubts go out the window. I fall fast asleep with a smile on my face.

Chapter Eight

*I*t's Monday morning, and the office is all abuzz talking about the Paris project. Nerves are setting in, and everyone seems a bit on edge.

I wish I could rewind the weekend and actually go out with Aiden. When I spoke to him yesterday, he still didn't sound good. I doubt he even came into the office today.

"I've already started packing," Bre says to Kimmy. I knew it. She's convinced one of those positions is hers. Yet no one has been interviewed. Bre's high opinion of herself never ceases to amaze me.

Kimmy and I exchange a glance, and she rolls her eyes. I try to hide my snicker, but Bre sees me.

"What's so funny, Erin?" she asks pointedly.

"Nothing," I say, shaking my head. "I was just appreciating your confidence."

She clearly doesn't like my answer. I think she's about to tell me how much she doesn't like my answer when Chelsie comes off the elevator. In an instant, the whole floor becomes completely silent. Is everyone holding their breath?

"You can all relax," she announces. "I just wanted to inform you that the interviews will begin tomorrow and will be held throughout the week. As I told you originally, only four people will be a part of the project. You'll be receiving an email later today with your interview time. Good luck everyone."

All at once there's a collective exhale as everyone starts to breathe again.

"This is so exciting," Aly squeals. She's been unusually quiet all morning until now.

Bre rolls her eyes in her direction. "Erin, can you look at this?" she asks, completely ignoring Aly. "My dating doctor sent me this email. What do you think?"

This is the Bre I know. A few minutes ago, she was getting defensive with me, and now she wants my advice on her dating life.

"You're still seeing the dating doctor?" I ask.

She gives me a confused look.

"You don't understand the process. Once a patient of Doctor D's, always a patient," she says knowingly.

She's right—I definitely don't understand this process. She's calling herself a patient, but is this guy actually a doctor?

"Doctor D will be by my side through my journey until I find my soul mate," she insists. "He has an amazing track record, and I trust him completely."

I skim through the doctor's email, and I have to admit it's very motivating and positive. It makes sense how she could become so engaged in this dating doctor program.

"Well? What do you think?"

Before I have a chance to answer her, Aly jumps up from her chair and claps. "I did it. I did it. They're interviewing me."

Bre and I stare at her and then glance at each other. *Holy crap!* She got her email. I practically dive on top of my laptop to open my emails, and there it is. I have an interview on Thursday.

The next few minutes seem like a blur. The office is filled with hopeful anticipation. I just have to continue reminding myself that we're not all going to Paris. There are four spots, and unlike Bre I want to remain *cautiously* optimistic.

"I think I'm in shock," Aly announces. "I never expected an opportunity like this with my first job."

Good for Aly. I would've loved a chance like this so early on in my career.

"Just remember we aren't there yet," Bre says, interrupting my thoughts. "We still have to convince the interview panel that we're the right people to represent *Strike a Pose*."

Bre is right, although I'm surprised she spoke to Aly at all and that she was actually civil. Usually she has a snarky comment or completely ignores her.

"Yes, I know," Aly says, an edge in her voice. "At least Aiden will be there during the interviews. His presence will definitely help with my nerves."

Wait, what?

"Erin, you have to be feeling very relieved about that," she adds.

Bre looks at me and raises her eyebrows.

"Not really," I say sharply. "There's a whole panel of people to convince."

Ugh. The last thing I want is for people to think that my personal relationship is the reason I get one of those positions.

"That's true, and some of them are tough," Bre adds. "Madeline Bufont is a force, and you know she will have the final word."

Bre picks up her bag and stands up.

"Anyway, I have to make a few calls, so I'm taking an early lunch."

Ha. In other words, we probably won't be seeing her for most of the day. She must be feeling very secure with her chances right now. And to her credit, Bre is a fantastic writer. If she only took a little more initiative to commit to her job, she'd be unstoppable.

I shoot Aiden a text letting him know about my interview.

Excellent news. I can't wait to celebrate with you.

My heart does a flip, and I smile to myself. For the first time in a while I feel like I'm finally moving forward.

~

After such an exciting day at the office, Kimmy, Bre, Aly, and I decide to meet for drinks to celebrate making it to the interview round. I'm in such a good mood, I actually feel like being social.

"Ahem," Kimmy says loudly, holding up her martini glass. It's filled to the rim with a bright pink beverage. "I want to make a toast. To the most talented gals around. I'm planning on saying a million Hail Mary's in hopes that we can all have drinks in Paris together. Cheers, ladies."

"Cheers," we all say in unison.

It's obvious that Bre already has a little buzz, especially when she puts her arm around Aly's shoulder and whispers something in her ear. Aly giggles, and you'd think the two of them are the best of friends. Hmm...I thought she didn't like Aly.

"Where's Aiden?" Bre teases. "Let's call him. He needs to grab his brother and join us. We have a lot to talk to him about."

I try to tell her he had food poisoning all weekend, but that doesn't stop her. Before I know it, she picks up her phone and starts scrolling.

"What are you doing?" I demand.

She gives me a wicked smile and waves her hand at me. She starts typing and then lets out a satisfied sigh when she's finished.

"Bre. What did you do?" I plead.

"Don't worry your pretty little head about anything, Erin. Auntie Bre took care of it." She rises to her feet and saunters toward the bathroom.

What? Who the hell is Auntie Bre? I glance at Aly, who's eyeing me curiously.

"Do you think Aiden will come down here?" Aly asks.

I feel a familiar wave of jealousy come over me, which is ridiculous. Aly is harmless, right?

"I'm not sure. He's been pretty sick," I tell her. "But Bre can be pretty relentless."

"Well, that would be cool if he stops by." She pauses. "So you two can spend time together."

I press my lips together. I'd like to believe that Aly's only interested is talking to Aiden about the interview process, but something just isn't sitting right. Crap. Maybe I'm overthinking this.

After about twenty minutes I'm starting to relax. Bre is so good at pushing buttons, and I know this. She's off flirting with a bartender while Aly, Kimmy, and I continue talking about Paris.

"Ohh, it looks like he made it," Kimmy exclaims.

I turn around to see Aiden rushing toward us.

"Erin, are you okay?" He's completely out of breath as if he ran the whole way here. What is he talking about?

"Yes, I'm perfectly fine." I place my hand on his shoulder. "Are you okay?"

"Bre texted Harry and told him that you needed help, so I rushed over."

He's breathing heavily, while I'm at a complete loss for words. And honestly, I don't know whether to kill Bre or hug her. Once again, her crazy shenanigans benefit me. That may not have been her intention, but I love that Aiden felt the need to rush to my rescue.

"I'm sorry she made you worry," I say softly. "I don't know what goes on in her head."

"So, you're okay?" he asks, reaching for my hand. An electric spark shoots through my body as soon as he touches me. His eyes lock on mine, and I suddenly wish we were somewhere else, alone.

"Erin's fine," Aly interrupts. "In fact, we're all doing great. We're celebrating."

Ugh. Can't she see we were having a moment?

"Yes, congrats to all of you," he says, not taking his eyes off of me.

"Thank goodness you're here, Aiden. We need to talk." Bre demands.

Of course Bre has to return at this moment along with her usual chaos. She's like a wrecking ball wherever she goes.

"Wait," I say. "I think you owe Aiden an apology for making him rush over here for no good reason."

"Yes, so sorry about that," she says unconvincingly. "Now can you give us any hints about these interviews? Anything we need to know going in."

Aiden gives her a frustrated look. "Bre, I'm one of five on a panel, and that's all I know at this point."

"Well, you're no help," Bre says glumly.

"Sorry. But good news for you, Harry's on his way over, so you can harass him when he gets here."

Bre folds her arms and pouts. "Harass him? That wasn't very nice."

"Well, you were the one who made me rush here to be with Erin, so that's what I'm going to do." He grabs my hand and leads me outside to the patio. I feel like I'm in a complete daze as his fingers tighten around mine.

"Finally," he says, wrapping his arms around me and kissing me on the forehead. "I should probably be thanking Bre for getting me here. At least it gives me a chance to see you. I felt so bad about canceling on Saturday."

"It's okay," I say looking up at him. "You're here now."

He runs his hands gently down my arms before pulling me toward him. Neither of us says another word as our lips touch. His kiss is different this time—it's fierce and passionate, and I willingly kiss him back.

"Look at my little brother go," a voice taunts. We let go of our embrace to see Harry watching us. "It looks like you're doing just fine, ET. Bre gave us quite a scare."

Aiden glares at him. "Get lost, Harrison."

Harry chuckles. Brothers can be so annoying sometimes.

"Bre is never subtle when it comes to getting what she wants," I tell him. "She wanted to get Aiden here, and she did. And look, you're here, too. Damn, she's good."

Harry shrugs his shoulders. "I respect a woman who goes after what she wants. Bre has an unshakeable fire in her, and I dig it."

Aiden and I glance at each other. It's clear that our moment is over.

"To be continued," he whispers.

He takes my hand in his and leads me back to my friends.

Aiden and Harry head to the bar, while Bre slides her chair closer to mine.

"So, are you mad at me for texting Harry?" she asks. "It seems to have worked out in your favor. I think the whole bar was watching your...um, conversation. That was pretty hot."

Heat fills my cheeks.

"I'm not mad at you, but you need to give Aiden a break about these interviews. You know he's not making the final decision."

Bre doesn't say anything. She's frowning at something behind me.

"Bre? Did you hear what I said?"

"Could she make it any more obvious," she says motioning behind me. When I turn around, I see Harry and Aiden at the bar with Aly. She's leaning in toward them and talking animatedly. All three of them start laughing.

"You have nothing to worry about," I insist. "Harry is definitely into you."

She nods her head. "Oh, I know, but I'm not talking about Harry. You better watch that girl around your man."

I glance back to see Aly put her arms around both Aiden's and Harry's shoulders. Hmm...I guess it won't hurt to keep an eye on her just in case.

Aiden, Aly, and I are the last to leave the restaurant. Ugh, why won't this girl get a hint. She's been talking Aiden's ear off about the magazine most of the night. Aiden, being the nice guy he is, continues to answer every question she has.

"It's getting late," Aiden says throwing a glance at me. "I'll walk you ladies to your cars."

"That's sweet of you," Aly replies. "Sorry about all the questions. Poor Erin has been dealing with this since I started at *Strike a Pose*."

I smile. "It's fine."

She continues to ramble as we walk outside.

"Aly, where are you parked?" Aiden asks immediately. I feel a sense of satisfaction that we're going to her car first. That will give us a few more minutes together without any interruptions. After Aly's safely on her way home, Aiden and I are finally alone.

"You're quite the gentleman, Aiden Thomas," I say.

He shrugs as he reaches for my hand. "Sometimes."

As soon as we arrive at my car, he doesn't waste any time picking up where we left off on the patio. When we finally stop kissing, we remain close for a moment longer, foreheads touching.

"I should probably let you get home," he says with hesitation.

I frown. "Yeah, I guess."

He pushes my hair behind my ear, cupping my cheek.

"Sweet dreams, ET."

He opens the door and places one more tender kiss on my forehead.

As I drive home, I realize that every time I see Aiden, I fall for him a little more, and I'm okay with that.

Chapter Nine

I've been on a lot of interviews in my life, and the preparation is always the same. The day before, I spend hours at Nordstrom trying to find the perfect outfit. And then I end up dropping a bunch of money on clothes, none of which I wear to my interview.

I've somehow managed to function, even though my head has been in the clouds since my encounter with Aiden in the empty parking lot. We've been texting nonstop, and I think it's safe to say that he's my boyfriend now. We haven't officially labeled our relationship, but it certainly feels like he is.

The big day has finally arrived, and I wake up extra early to give myself time to get ready, as opposed to every other day when I rush around. I choose a V-neck black dress that comes right above my knees and pair it with black stilettos. When all else fails, the shoes need to be on point. I know the shoes aren't going to get me the job, but I just really like them.

After thinking about it, I realize how silly it is to obsess about this interview. No matter what happens, I have a job I enjoy, and I'll still have it even if I don't get chosen to go to Paris. There's no reason for me to be so frazzled. Kimmy already had her interview yesterday. She said they gave her a few topics and she had to brainstorm some ideas for articles. Normally I'm pretty good with brainstorming, but I'm not sure how I'll do with five sets of eyes on me, including Aiden's.

"Well, don't you look hot today," Bre says when she strolls in at ten o'clock. Technically no one is paying attention to when we arrive at the office, but Bre's the only one who seems to have an issue getting here at eight a.m. She definitely likes to make her own rules.

"You really don't need to try so hard," she adds with a smirk. After all, you only need to impress four members of the panel."

I roll my eyes and let out a sigh. "Whatever, Bre. Perhaps you should worry about your own job? A little late today, aren't you?"

She glares at me but doesn't respond. That's because she knows I'm right.

Aly continues to prance around the office like she's been here for years. She doesn't seem the slightest bit worried or nervous. It seems her newfound confidence is here to stay.

Meanwhile I'm on pins and needles until it's officially time for my interview. As soon as I walk into the conference room, my heart starts to speed up. Of course I manage to trip on a piece of cheap carpet as soon as I enter the room. Ugh, nothing like making a grand entrance. My clumsiness appears at the most unfortunate of times. Thankfully I catch myself and try to laugh it off.

When I see Aiden, a feeling of calmness settles in. He looks me up and down, and his mouth drops open.

The interview begins with introductions and some details about what the job will entail.

"Ms. Taylor, your work is rather brilliant," Madeline Bufont says, looking through a folder. She has a slight British accent which makes me want to be best friends with her. "I'm most impressed."

I can feel my shoulders relax a little. A compliment from Ms. Bufont is worth all the stress and second-guessing of my abilities to put together a decent article.

Each person on the panel asks a different question. I notice that the questions all involve me using my own creativity with different topics including self-esteem, trends, and social situations. The panel clearly wants to know how I can reach readers, and I'm actually impressed with my answers so far.

When it comes time for Aiden's turn, he gives me a warm smile.

"Thank you for being here today, Ms. Taylor," he says professionally. I can feel my face getting red, but I'm trying my best to stay a hundred percent focused on the interview.

"I'm glad to be here," I reply. Aiden's casually leaning back in his chair, and I notice he's wearing a suit coat with the top button of his shirt open.

Gah. *Focus, Erin.*

I methodically answer his question, not missing a beat despite noticing how handsome he looks.

The final question is from Madeline Bufont. She asks me why I want to be part of this project.

I don't look at Aiden because all of a sudden the idea of being away from him for two months makes my heart sink into my stomach.

I exhale slowly before giving my answer.

"I've been at *Strike a Pose* for two years, and I'm ready to take my career to the next level." I pause. "Journalism is my passion. Writing is the only thing I've ever wanted to do and an opportunity to learn from everyone at *Bleu Amour* would be the chance of a lifetime. I'm also confident in my abilities to enhance your team in Paris with my experiences and knowledge." I stop talking and flash a bright smile.

"Very good, Ms. Taylor," she says with a slight nod.

I'm assuming that means she's satisfied with my answer, but you never know.

"We'll be in touch once we've met with all of the candidates and made our decision."

I practically jump up from my chair, and all the members of the panel stand as well. I walk over to shake their hands. One by one they thank me for coming in. When I get to Aiden, he smiles and takes my hand in his tight grip. Feeling my hand in his makes my head spin. "Great interview, Ms. Taylor."

In this moment, I consider yelling out, "Forget Paris," and kissing him, but instead I just smile and let out a deep sigh.

Let the waiting game begin.

"It couldn't have gone better," Aly exclaims. "I feel like I didn't miss a beat. They told me how impressed they were with my article and my writing is like that of a well-seasoned journalist."

It's Friday afternoon, and she hasn't stopped talking about her interview all day. I'd bet money that everyone else in the office is just as over it. Bre had her interview before Aly earlier this morning and took an early lunch to celebrate how well she did (her words.)

"That's great news," I say, straightening up my desk. I'm trying to continue being a cheerleader for her, but my patience is wearing thin. Her growing ego should be enough to constantly boost her up.

After such a crazy week, nothing could put a bigger damper on it than having to go to my brother's birthday dinner tonight. Liza has planned the whole celebration, and it'll probably be bigger than my niece's party. Does a thirty-one-year-old man really need a huge party? Not usually, but this is my brother we're talking about.

"We should go out and celebrate tonight," Aly suggests. Hmm...I'm not sure which would be worse, listening to Aly talk about her interview all night or being around my brother who thinks the world should revolve around him because he was born.

I groan. "As much as I'd love to do that, I have a family event to attend."

I don't think I sound very convincing, but it is what it is.

"Oh, okay," she says, her face falling. This makes me wonder if she has any other friends. It occurs to me that I really don't know much about Aly at all.

After I leave the office, I make my way toward my brother's house. I spend the journey mentally preparing myself for a thrilling evening with my family. In a pinch, I can always talk about work, which is a topic I'd prefer to discuss rather than my relationships. I'm sure my mother will have plenty to say about Will and how she's decided that he and I are meant to live happily ever after with one another. She never acted like this when it came to Eric's relationships. He had a few girlfriends prior to Liza, and I think my mother approved of most of them. Although there isn't much my mother doesn't support when it comes to my brother.

I pull up into Eric's driveway and take a few extra minutes to do some breathing exercises.

When I'm finally ready, I let myself in and follow the sounds of music and voices. My brother's backyard is absolutely breathtaking at this time of night with the sun setting behind the mountains. For a brief moment I considered inviting Aiden tonight, but things are going so well that I didn't want one evening with my family to scare him away.

"Happy birthday, old man," I announce as soon as I see my brother.

He scowls before putting his arm across my shoulders.

"You're hilarious," he says. "I'll remember that in a few years when you're my age."

"Was there any doubt?" I ask with an exaggerated eye roll. My brother will look for any excuse to tease me, the only leg I have up is that I'm younger than him.

He quickly abandons me to greet a few of his friends so I head to the bar and order a Diet Coke.

"Hi there, sweet pie." My dad says coming up beside me.

"Hi, Daddy," I say, giving him a big hug. "Where did you come from?"

"We just got here," he says, putting his hands on my shoulders.

I give him a curious look. "We?"

He shifts from one foot to another.

"Your mother and I came together," he says nonchalantly.

Huh? My parents are so weird. Don't get me wrong, I'm glad they're still friends…if that's all they really are.

"Oh really?" I ask playfully, elbowing him in the side.

"Very funny. You can just get those crazy thoughts out of your head," he says, the corner of his mouth curling into a smile.

I shrug innocently. "Sure, whatever you say."

My dad's cheeks turn a shade of pink, and my mom joins us.

"I was wondering where you ran off to, Edward. Hello, honey," she says, giving me a side hug.

"So, Dad says you two came to the party together."

She gives me a blank stare. "What's wrong with that? It's our son's birthday. And speaking of which, tonight is about him, so let's focus on that.

She grabs our hands and pulls my dad and me toward the house. She won't get any complaints out of me. The sooner we get this party started, the quicker it ends.

Two hours into the party and not a single mention of Will. Just when I think I'm in the clear, my mother brings him up as I'm about to devour a huge piece of Liza's amazing chocolate cake.

"Mom, I've told you that Will and I are just friends."

Her face falls, and I can see how disappointed she is. "Anyway, I'd much rather talk about you..." I pause. "And Dad."

She clears her throat. "I'm not sure what you're referring to. We're here celebrating our son. That isn't exactly unusual."

I give her a doubtful look. "It's not unusual, but you two seem closer all of a sudden, even closer than when you were married."

Her jaw tightens. I guess she doesn't like it when the roles are reversed. She certainly has no problem badgering me about my personal life.

"Erin, there's nothing to discuss. We're still a family despite choosing to end our marriage," she exclaims. I shake my head and let out an exasperated sigh.

Fortunately Liza interrupts at exactly the right moment. "Come along, ladies. It's time for presents."

My mother is visibly thrilled to be out of the hot seat. I wander into the parlor where the guests have gathered around my brother. It's actually the living room, but Eric and Liza insist on calling it a parlor—how very pretentious of them.

I sit down on one of the huge fluffy couches and pull out my phone. My stomach does a flip when I see two text messages from Aiden waiting for me.

I'm bored.

Want to hang out tonight?

Hah, like he has to ask. I quickly respond.

Sure. At a family party now, but I was looking for an excuse to get out of here.

My heart continues to beat rapidly as I wait for him to reply.

Eric unwraps his first gift, a new Rolex watch from Liza— because he needed another one, naturally. Last I heard he already had two. He passionately kisses Liza, and the crowd cheers while I want to tell them to get a room. My phone buzzes again, and a smile spreads across my face as I read the message.

I'll gladly be your excuse. I can come over if you want, or you can come here.

I text him back inviting him to meet me at my apartment in an hour. Thankfully, his texts help me through the torture of watching Eric open presents. You would think my brother was eight years old.

As soon as the party starts to die down, I'm the first to make my exit. I quickly hug my family and practically race to my car.

On my way home I call Mia.

"I just had to endure hours of Eric's birthday party," I whine.

She laughs.

"Oh fun...what did he get? A Mercedes? An island in the Caribbean?"

I laugh. "Not this time. Maybe next year. In other news Aiden's coming over.

"Ah, now that sounds a lot more fun than an evening of worshiping your brother," she exclaims.

"Yeah, you could say that." I giggle.

Before we hang up, she makes me promise to call her after Aiden leaves. I remind her of the time zone difference, but she still insists I at least send her a text with a detailed description of our evening. It's possible she's as excited about what's happening with Aiden as I am. Well, maybe.

Clueless is one of my favorite movies of all time. I love the part where Alicia Silverstone's character invites a guy over, picks out her sexiest outfit, and drops an entire roll of cookie dough on a baking sheet. It's a great idea in theory, but I have no intention of prancing around in a trampy little dress or attempting to have any baked goods waiting for Aiden. Instead, I pick out my favorite yoga pants along with a pink tank top. I put some cheese and crackers on a serving plate, make sure I have a variety of drinks in the fridge, and finish getting ready.

I'm straightening pillows on my couches when I hear a knock. I run my fingers through my hair and casually walk to the door. I take a deep cleansing breath as I open it.

Aiden must've been thinking the same thing as me. He's wearing Adidas workout pants and a tight T-shirt that says *Stop Staring.*

Really, of all the shirts he could've worn.

"Nice shirt," I say with a smirk.

He looks down and shrugs. "Are you staring?"

Um, hello. Of course I'm staring.

I shrug my shoulders. "I'll never tell."

He laughs as I hold the door open for him. As soon as he walks through the door, he leans over and kisses me on the cheek. My face gets hot at the touch of his lips.

"This is a great place, and the view is phenomenal," he exclaims, moving toward the window.

"Thanks," I say, joining him. "I fell in love with this apartment as soon as I saw it."

We both stand silently and look out over the twinkling lights of our city skyline.

"So, can I get you a drink?" I ask a few seconds later. "I have wine, Diet Coke, water, Yoo-hoo."

A grin spreads across his face. "Did you just say Yoo-hoo? Really?"

"Yeah," I say folding my arms tightly against my chest. "Don't judge me. It's my favorite drink of all time, even though it has about a thousand grams of sugar in one bottle."

Aiden nods while smirking.

"What?" I ask.

"Nothing," he says innocently. "I was just thinking that I'd like to try a Yoo-hoo. I think I was nine years old the last time I had one. Why not live a little dangerously tonight?" He closes his lips tightly to keep his laughter from escaping.

I scowl. "Very funny."

When I return from the kitchen, I find Aiden sitting casually on my couch, looking at his phone. He looks so perfect here in my living room. I wish I could take a picture and send it to Mia. I sit down next to him and hand him his Yoo-hoo. Our hands touch as he reaches for his drink which causes an electric shock to shoot through my body.

He takes a sip and then holds up the bottle. "Damn, I forgot how good this stuff is."

I smile. "I always have them in stock, but believe it or not, I don't drink them that often. I just like to have them in case of an emergency."

He nods. "Of course. There's nothing like kicking back with a Yoo-hoo after a hard day."

I roll my eyes. "Ha-ha."

He leans back and puts his arm on the back of the couch behind me. "Thanks for inviting me over. I'm sorry if I pulled you away from your family party."

I shake my head. "Believe me, your interruption couldn't have been more perfect. Of course I love my family, but there's only so much celebrating of my brother I can take."

"I totally get it, believe me," he announces.

He begins to play with a few strands of my hair, which is my favorite thing ever.

"Anyway, I'd rather not spend the evening talking about complicated family relationships."

He smiles. "Yes, I'd much rather talk about you."

I laugh. "Are you sure? Nights filled with TV watching and Yoo-hoo aren't super exciting."

"Sounds like a great evening to me, especially with the right person," he adds.

As we talk we continue to move closer to one another. I pull my knees into me, and he places his hand on them. Before I know it, we're practically intertwined, and it feels perfect. We talk about our favorite movies, interests, and thankfully the interview doesn't come up. As much as I'd love to know what the panel said about me, I don't want to put him in an awkward position.

I try to hold in my yawns because I don't want this evening to end.

"Aw, you're sleepy. I should go," he whispers.

I nod sadly, but neither of us moves from our positions on the couch. "I'm glad you came over."

He looks into my eyes. "Me too."

Our faces are a few inches apart, and I want more than anything for him to kiss me. He must read my mind because all of a sudden he pulls me into his lap.

I don't waste any time before I wrap my arms around his neck and kiss him. Normally, I'd let him make all the moves, but this just feels like the right thing to do. His arms are wrapped tightly around my waist, and the moment is intensifying rapidly.

"I probably should go," he says without pulling his lips away from mine.

"Mm-hmm."

When I finally pry myself away from him to catch my breath, we both lean our heads back on the couch.

"Wow, ET, you really know how to make your guests feel welcome," he says, giving me a mischievous grin.

I playfully punch him on the arm. "Hey now, I believe you were the one who pulled me into your lap."

"Yes, but I didn't detect any hesitation from you. And you look so amazing tonight, I'd be stupid not to try to make a move on you. What would my friends say?"

I let out a giggle. "I see your point."

"Anyway, I really better get going, or I may never leave," Aiden says, kissing my hand.

That's fine with me.

After we walk to the door, he pulls me into his arms and lifts me off the ground while kissing me.

"When can I see you again?" he asks urgently as he gently places me down on the floor.

"You'll see me at work on Monday," I remind him. I know that's not what he meant.

"Well, yes. But I'm talking about a repeat of tonight."

I give him a coy smile. "The sooner the better."

He kisses me three more times and touches his forehead against mine. "That's what I was hoping you'd say. Good night, Erin."

I close the door behind him and lean up against it as if I'm in some swoony romantic comedy movie. I skip off to the kitchen to clean up and get ready for bed, although I have no idea how I'm going to fall asleep after such a perfect evening with Aiden. I don't want this feeling to go away. Ever.

Chapter Ten

"*I* can't believe you didn't text me. I stayed up all night waiting for your call," Mia whines. "I was going to call, but I didn't want to interrupt you and your new man."

"Oh, whatever," I say, rubbing my eyes. It's super early, and of course I didn't get to sleep until the wee hours of the morning. I stayed up watching *Friends* reruns because I was too excited to sleep.

"So, are you going to give me the scoop or what?" she asks impatiently.

I can barely hold my eyes open. "Ugh. It's five-thirty, *Pacific* time. Can I call you back in a few hours? I'm exhausted."

"Oh really, and why is that?" she teases. *Seriously? It's way too early for this.* Although the idea of reliving my evening with Aiden is enticing.

"You might as well start talking now because you know how impatient I am, and I'll just keep calling you back," she reminds me.

This is true. And now that I'm starting to wake up, I'm remembering every perfect moment of last night.

"It was...so good," I say softly. I give her all the details and wait for her to give me her two cents. She doesn't say anything, and for a second I think we got disconnected.

"Mia? You there?" I ask.

"I'm here," she says finally. "I was just thinking that it sounds like you're falling in love with Aiden."

What?

"Have you gone mad? No. I mean I really like him, but that's a bit premature."

"Uh-huh."

"I promise you'll be the first to know if I fall in love."

"Okay," she says. "When are you seeing him again?"

"Monday at work."

"Boo. That's lame," she wails. "Call me if something exciting happens."

"Always," I say. "But not at five a.m."

"I'll be awake."

I laugh. "Yeah, but that would be two a.m. here, so no."

As soon as we end the call, I think about what Mia said. There's no doubt in my mind that my feelings for Aiden are strong, but how strong are they?

~

When I arrive at the office on Monday morning, I feel confident and excited. I took my time getting ready and making sure I look put together. I must be pretty transparent because Bre notices right away.

"Damn, girl, you look great," she says, giving me the once-over. "Any special reason? Or should I say, special person."

"No. I don't need a reason to dress up for work," I say, looking down at my dark skinny jeans, ankle books, and black tunic. I don't think my outfit is obvious at all, and I refuse to let her make me paranoid. "I know this may shock you, but not everyone's purpose in life is to impress men."

She rolls her eyes, but she knows I'm right. "Anyway, in a few weeks, you and I will be sipping champagne along the Champs-Élysées. Isn't it exciting?"

"We'll see. That would be fantastic." I cross two fingers on both hands.

There's a part of me that wishes I had Bre's level of confidence about going to Paris. Maybe she's manifesting it to happen.

I sit down at my desk and open my laptop. I'm trying very hard to concentrate on my work. I put in my earbuds to make it look like I'm in the zone. This also helps drown out Bre and Aly, who are talking nonstop about Paris. I see my phone light up, and my heart starts to race expecting it to be a text from

Aiden. Unfortunately it's not from Aiden—it's a message from Will.

Hey, stranger. When are we hanging out? Coffee? Brunch?

I haven't spoken to Will since we went out.

Hey. Sorry. Work has been crazy. Coffee sounds good.

Is this weird? It shouldn't be, right? It's coffee with a friend. And Aiden and I haven't exactly labeled our relationship, nor have we said we're exclusive. Will and I text back a few more times and agree to meet sometime this week. I don't think you can get any closer to the friend zone than having coffee with someone.

"Who are you texting?" Aly teases. "Judging by the smile on your face—it must be Aiden."

All of sudden, Bre's warning about Aly pops into my mind.

I turn to her and casually slip my phone into my bag. "Nope. It's just a friend I haven't seen in a while," I reply.

"Oh, cool. By the way, Aiden is the best. He was so welcoming and patient during my interview."

And there's that wave of jealousy again. Why do I feel like she's purposely trying push my buttons?

"Yes, Aiden is pretty amazing," I gush. We both grow quiet. I'm not sure why our conversation has become uncomfortable—but it has. It's pretty clear that Aly has a bit of a crush on Aiden. And honestly, who could blame her. Unfortunately for her, he's made it very clear how he feels about me, and all the obvious flirting she's putting out isn't going to change that.

Thankfully Kimmy rushes off the elevator, interrupting our awkward conversation. "Guess what I just heard. They're ready to make an announcement about the team," she squeals. "Could you imagine if we all get to go together?"

"That would be so great," Aly says. "I wonder if we'll be in hotel rooms or maybe they'll put us in an apartment together?"

I let a snort escape from my mouth as I envision Bre and Aly living together for two months. The image of stuffed animals and alarms going off at five a.m. flash through my mind.

As fun as it is to daydream about what life in Paris would be like, none of us know if we have the job.

I hold up my hand. "I hate to break up all the planning, but let's just wait for the announcement."

I turn back to my laptop, while Kimmy and Aly ignore my request. I should probably get used to this until the day the team leaves. Hopefully I'm one of them.

I open my eyes and look around my living room. I'm still in my work clothes and my bags are on the floor where I dropped them when I came home. I can't believe I fell asleep on the couch. Holy crap, I must've been more tired than I thought. I jump up to find my phone, and my heart speeds up when I see a missed call from Aiden about an hour ago.

I immediately call him back.

"Hey," he answers on the first ring.

"Hi. I'm glad you're still up," I say. "I passed out on the couch when I got home, and I just woke up. I'm not going to be able to sleep tonight."

"Hmm...someone must've kept you up late last night. You should have a talk with that person."

"I should," I exclaim. "Anyway, how was your day?"

"Busy. I can't wait for this international project to be over. This panel is taking up a lot of my time." He sounds exhausted.

"I'm sorry," I say. "I'm sure it's a difficult process. I hope I'm not complicating things." I grit my teeth while waiting for his response. This is exactly why I haven't asked him anything about the interviews. My feelings for him have nothing to do with this project.

"No, it's not you at all," he insists. "Please don't let that thought get into your mind. You and I are—well, I like where things are going. And I really like you."

I feel my face grow hot. I'm glad he's not here to see me blush.

"Good, because I feel the same way."

Honestly at this point I'm ready for the announcement to be made, no matter what the outcome is. Which makes me wonder—how do I feel about the possibility of leaving Aiden for two months. Wow. Timing really is everything.

"It's good to see you, buddy," Will says cheerfully.

We both start to laugh. I've actually been looking forward to hanging out with Will again. He really is a lot of fun, almost like the brother I wish I had. Not that I don't love my brother, but Will is so much more easygoing than Eric.

"If Margie and Sharon could see us now," he says after we sit down at our table.

"Seriously, could you imagine?" I reply. "You didn't tell your mom about us meeting for coffee, did you?"

Will gives me a curious look. "Of course I did. You know I'm all about pleasing my mother, and if it gets her to stop nagging me—so be it."

I give him a curious look. "Sometimes I don't know when you're being serious," I say with a giggle.

"That's all part of my charm. I was actually going to tell you that she paid me to keep seeing you."

I roll my eyes.

"I'm kidding, although that gives me an idea," he says.

"I think we've been dealing with enough brilliant ideas already."

He nods swiftly. "Amen to that." He takes a sip of his coffee. "Enough about that. How's life? Are you still seeing that guy you were telling me about?"

"Yes," I say, trying to tone down my excitement. "Except the timing isn't ideal."

"Uh-oh, why?"

I tell him about the Paris project and Aiden being on the interview panel.

"So he had to interview you for this job? Was that awkward?"

"Not at all," I say. "He asked a question, and I gave my answer —very professionally."

"Damn, I bet that was hard for him."

I frown. "For him? I was the one being interviewed."

"Yeah, but he had to try not to check you out. You're pretty hot, Erin."

I giggle and blush at the same time. "Well, thanks."

"Erinnnn," a high pitched voice squeals.

I turn around to see Aly and another girl sitting at the table right behind us. Of course Aly's eyes are fixated on Will. I can only imagine what she's thinking.

"Hey, Aly," I say cheerfully. She gives me a wicked smile, and then her eyes shift right back to Will.

"This is my friend Will," I say, pointing at him. I try not to be too obvious as I emphasize the word friend, but I feel like I need to make it clear in case she's getting any wild ideas.

"Aly works with me at *Strike a Pose*," I tell Will. She doesn't try to hide the fact that she's sizing him up, and I can't help but worry about her running her mouth at the office. Will and I are friends, but she could spin it any way she wants.

"Great to meet you, Aly," Will says. "Are you a journalist as well?"

She nods eagerly, and it's obvious that she's about to explode if she doesn't talk about her job.

"I sure am," she says proudly. "I actually just graduated, and this is my first job. Thankfully, Erin has been there to help me." She looks over at her friend, who's too busy on her phone to even look up. "This is my friend Tara."

Tara glances up long enough to say hello.

Aly's attention has quickly returned back to Will and me. "So, how do you guys know each other?" I look at Will, expecting him to chime in, but he doesn't say anything. Is he waiting for me to answer her question? If one of us doesn't speak up, it's going to seem like we have something to hide.

"Our mothers are best friends," I reply. "At least they are this week. Of course, that could change at any moment."

"Good point," he agrees, leaning back in his chair. "Can one of you please explain why women talk about each other behind their backs? Even women they claim are their friends. I know it's a random question, but I'm just curious."

"That would be one of life's greatest mysteries," I say in a dramatic voice.

Will seems intrigued.

"But why?" he asks.

Ha, does he really want to get into a topic like this? It's pretty deep, like politics or religion.

"Honestly, I don't know," I answer finally. "I guess something drives women to want to prove they can measure up. Jealousy? Ego? What do you think, Aly?"

I can almost see the wheels turning in her head.

"I don't think it's always bad. Sometimes it's just flattery," she says thoughtfully.

Will looks at me and raises his eyebrows.

Seriously? I hardly consider talking bad about someone a form of flattery, but to each his own.

She must notice my reaction, so she continues talking. "I'm just saying that everyone does it—and it doesn't always mean the person isn't a good friend."

Will looks as confused as I feel.

Fortunately our conversation is cut short when Aly's phone rings. We continue talking about life, and Will tells me he got tickets to one of the NBA playoff games.

"I'd ask you to join me, but these are excellent seats and we already friend zoned each other," he says with a wink.

Out of the corner of my eye I can see that Aly is still carefully watching us like she's a private investigator. I almost expect her to pull out a pad of paper and take notes.

I laugh. "I understand."

"Do you hear that sound?" He asks, holding his hand up to his ear. "It's the sound of Margie's and Sharon's hearts breaking. They might disown us."

I let out a giggle. "Possibly, but they'll survive."

On our way out, we say good-bye to Aly and her friend and head outside.

It's a cloudy and chilly afternoon, so I zip up my leather jacket.

"So, what's Aly's story," Will asks.

"Good question."

I tell him about the sweet and innocent Aly who first arrived at *Strike a Pose* and how she's turned into an overconfident, manipulative coworker overnight.

"She seemed pretty interested in our friendship."

I nod. "You noticed that too?"

I almost blurt out how much it bothers me when she openly flirts with Aiden, but I hold back.

"My friend Bre hasn't trusted her from day one. She insists there's more to Aly than what she portrays."

Will is listening intensely, or at least it seems like he's listening. His eyes are hidden behind a pair of very expensive sunglasses.

"Am I boring you?" I ask.

He cracks a smile. "Of course not."

"Sorry. Girl drama can be annoying."

He leans into me. "Believe it or not, I find girl drama fascinating. Growing up with three sisters will do that to you. Day after day it was another ridiculous issue with backstabbing friends, broken hearts, and some nonsense about wearing the same prom dress."

Wow. I think I've found my new best friend. Having a male friend to talk about these things with is probably a good idea because they can listen rationally and not be emotional. "Wow, I'm so impressed by you right now."

Will's face lights up. "I know, I'm pretty great. And I think Aly seems harmless. But sometimes those are the ones to watch. I wouldn't let your guard down completely."

That's exactly what I needed to hear—for some reason it sounds different coming from Will. Maybe because he has nothing to gain from it. And from now on my guard is staying up when it comes to Aly.

Chapter Eleven

*U*gh. Oversleeping really stresses me out especially right now with so much going on at the magazine. I'm so frazzled about being late that I almost leave my apartment wearing two different shoes. Thankfully, I figure it out before I dash out the door. Not that anyone would notice since most of my coworkers are on the edge of their seats waiting for the big announcement. Chelsie said we should be hearing any day, and I'm just ready to know so I can move on with my life one way or another.

It's kind of difficult to concentrate right now because the office is abuzz with talk of the project.

"What are you going to do if you aren't selected?" Kimmy asks Bre.

What is she doing? Hasn't she ever heard the saying *Don't throw rocks at the bear?*

Both Aly and I are listening for Bre's response.

Bre lets out a sharp laugh but doesn't have a chance to respond before Chelsie steps off the elevator. There's a collective gasp in the room followed by silence. Here we go.

"Good morning, there will be a meeting in conference room in fifteen minutes. Madeline Bufont is making the announcement," Chelsie says.

Ahhh, the moment of truth. The next fifteen minutes will feel like an eternity.

The office grows quiet while we anxiously wait for the meeting to start. I try to make myself busy instead of watching the clock, but I'm unsuccessful.

After what feels like fifteen *hours*, we finally make our way to the conference room and sit down. It's so quiet you could hear a pin drop. No one is speaking, and almost everyone looks like they're on the verge of a panic attack. Everyone except Bre—who's scrolling through her phone like she doesn't have a care in the world.

Chelsie sits down at the head of the table and types something on her laptop. I hold my breath as I wait for Madeline Bufont to join us remotely.

"Madeline, are you there?" Chelsie asks.

"Bonjour," she answers. Her video is turned off, but I just love her sophisticated British accent. Madeline is so elegant. It would be such an amazing experience to work closely with her for a few months.

"I have our team here," Chelsie says. "They're anxiously awaiting the decision." I look around the table. Bre is now picking at her nail polish, Kimmy and Sean have plastered fake smiles on their faces, and Aly has her hands in prayer position.

"*Merci a tous,*" she sings. "We have seen so much talent, but unfortunately we can't bring you all on. Please keep in mind that if this project goes well, we may have more opportunities in the future."

That's definitely good news.

"After much discussion and review, we have selected our new team. It will consist of three from your department and one person from the art department. Welcome to our team, Aly Sanders, Sean Wilson, and Erin Taylor."

That's me. They chose me.

I glance around the room. Aly is fanning her face with her hands, Kimmy congratulates Sean, and Bre is frozen in her seat. She has no expression, no anger, no tears.

"Bre, are you okay?" I ask cautiously.

"Congrats, Erin, and to you all," she says as she gets up from her chair and walks quickly out of the room.

"We did it, Erin," Aly says excitedly. I nod and smile. I do feel badly for Bre though, and I'm a little surprised by her reaction. It wasn't quite what I expected from her—it was too calm.

The rest of us try to settle down and listen to a few more instructions from Madeline before Chelsie ends the call. She congratulates us on a job well done and excuses us to return to work.

"Is Bre all right?" Aly asks as we make our way back to our desks. Her concern doesn't fool me. She may be acting like she cares, but I know she's gloating on the inside. Bre hasn't exactly been nice to her.

"I'm sure she'll be fine," I reply.

When I get back to my desk, I text Aiden. There's a part of me that feels like a weight has been lifted off my shoulders now the announcement has been made. I'm about to call my mother and give her my good news when I get a reply from Aiden asking me to have dinner with him tonight.

Of course there's no one I'd rather celebrate with.

I notice that Bre's bag is gone, so I'm assuming she's left for the day. Her pride may be a little hurt, but Bre's resilient. I'm sure she'll be okay.

"This is a dream come true," Aly exclaims, spinning around in her chair. "I feel like we owe Aiden a huge thank you."

Ugh, it really irks me when she says this. It's not like Aiden made the final decision.

"I don't think so," I reply. "We earned this on our own merit."

She nods quickly.

"Oh, sure, but you know what I'm saying."

I lean my head to the side. "No, I don't."

"Aiden was on the panel," she reminds me. "I'm sure he gave his recommendations."

"Maybe," I say with a shrug.

"By the way, it was fun running into you yesterday," she says giving me a wicked smile. "Will seems great."

My jaw tightens.

"Yes, he's a good friend," I reply.

"Oh, I know," she says innocently. "I wasn't trying to imply anything."

Hmmm...wasn't she? I know exactly what she was implying, but I refuse to give her the satisfaction of getting me fired up. I don't have to defend my friendships to her or anyone else.

As the day goes on, I make every effort to ignore Aly. Of course, it's almost impossible because she's been on the phone all day telling everyone she knows about being selected for the project. Thankfully Bre never returns to the office. I send her two texts asking if she's okay, but she hasn't responded.

At five o'clock sharp, Aiden saunters off the elevator looking as dashing as ever. I feel like it's been an eternity since he was with me at my apartment. Unfortunately, Aly is still hanging around, and she practically pounces on him as soon as she sees him.

"Aiden, isn't it exciting that Erin and I will be in Paris together?"

"Yes, congratulations," he says, flashing one of his signature smiles.

"Thanks for putting in a good word for us," she adds nudging him with her elbow.

He shakes his head. "I didn't do anything. Your talents and work ethic earned you those spots."

"Well, you're sweet," she coos.

"I'm ready when you are," I announce loudly, startling Aly out of her schoolgirl dreamy-eyed stare.

"Excellent," Aiden says, flashing me the same gorgeous smile he just gave Aly.

It's not a competition, Erin.

We finally escape Aly's clutches and head down the street to a quaint family-owned Italian restaurant. We both remain quiet as we walk, which is unusual for us. For some reason it feels different from the last time we were together. I want to ask him if anything is bothering him, but I don't want to pry.

"I'm sure you're relieved the interviews are over, right?" I ask as soon as we're seated.

"Definitely." He pauses and exhales loudly like he's about to unload some huge secret on me.

"Honestly, I knew you'd be a front-runner for the job but was afraid our relationship might interfere, so I've been trying to avoid the subject."

I love hearing him mention our *relationship*. I try not to react even though I want to jump up on the table and dance.

"I totally understand," I say, feeling a huge sense of relief wash over me. "I'm sure it put you in an awkward position as well, and I hope that I didn't add any extra pressure on you. And I'm especially sorry about Bre and Aly. I told them multiple times that you weren't the only person making the decision."

He shakes his head. "You didn't do anything wrong. Sure, Bre drives me crazy, but I'm used to it. I'm just glad it's over and we can move on." He reaches over and grabs my hand, sending shivers down my spine.

"Me, too," I say softy.

He doesn't let go of my hand until our food comes out. I can't believe I'm getting this excited over him holding my hand. I feel like I'm in the eighth grade.

"I have to make a confession," he says after the server brings us our coffee. "I briefly considered not giving you my vote, but only for purely selfish reasons."

I give him a confused look as he continues talking. "Of course I want you to enjoy every opportunity this project presents, but the thought of you running off to France for two months makes me really sad. What if some French guy comes along and sweeps you off your feet?"

For some reason, I immediately think about *Emily in Paris* and her super hot French neighbor. This TV addiction must be worse than I thought. Maybe my mother is right? I probably do need to get out more.

"You don't need to worry about that," I tell him. " I'm sure I'll be too busy to even think about having a social life."

"I don't know," he says. "I've heard rumors that the staff at *Bleu Amour* can get a little wild. And Aly told Harry and I that she had an itinerary all planned out for you ladies and that you were going to take Paris by storm."

"Did she?" I say curiously. "This is news to me."

Ugh, I'm growing more and more tired of Aly.

Aiden looks confused. "She told us when we ran into you on your girl's night out. Of course, it was before you were chosen for the positions."

"I think she was getting ahead of herself," I explain. "I mean, we briefly talked about it over drinks, but considering we hadn't gotten the jobs yet, that would've been extremely presumptuous. Although there was a lot of that going around —mostly from Bre."

He makes a face.

"Are you allowed to tell me what happened with Bre's interview, or is that off-limits?"

He shakes his head and takes a sip of his water. "Not much to tell, really. She did excellent in her interview, but the panel wasn't as impressed with her article. It wasn't bad by any means. It just wasn't as good as some of the other submissions."

Well, that's not as interesting as I expected it to be.

"How was she after the announcement was made?" he asks.

"She was quiet," I exclaim. "Oddly quiet, actually. I'm sure she's taking it hard. I texted her, but she hasn't responded to me."

"She'll get over it," he retorts. "There will be a new crisis tomorrow, and Paris will be a distant memory."

I nod. "You're probably right."

We don't talk about Bre for very long, and after dinner we take our time walking to my car, our hands clasped.

"When can I see you again?" he asks wrapping his arms around my waist. "I feel like I need to soak up as much time with you as I can before you leave for Paris."

"I think we can make that happen," I say running my hands over his biceps.

"How about this weekend?" he asks. "I could make you dinner as long as you understand that I'm an average chef at best."

I wonder what he would think if I did a few cartwheels right here in the parking lot.

"I'd love it, and I have a feeling you aren't average at anything you do," I say, running my fingers through his hair. "I can bring dessert."

A huge smile spreads across his face. "Yes, please do."

"That's fantastic," Mia squeals. "I'm already planning my visit."

I knew she'd say that.

"Have you told Mama Margie yet?" she asks with a snicker.

"Not yet, but hopefully it gives her something to brag to her friends about rather than my love life."

She giggles. "Let's hope."

"I'm not sure how much free time I'll have while I'm there. Remember this isn't a vacation. I'll be working."

"Yeah, yeah," Mia says, barely listening. "It'll be a blast, business trip or not."

This is true. Mia and I can have fun going to the dentist if we're together.

"Okay. Jack just got home, and he's requesting some attention from me. Keep me posted on the dates and details."

"I will," I tell her.

As much as I tried to downplay it, I'm ecstatic about going to Paris, even if I end up working the entire time. Seeing the City of Lights in person is a dream come true. The only thing that could make it perfect would be having Aiden there with me.

For the first time in forever, I don't even turn on the TV. I open my laptop and start planning my two months in France. Maybe Aly has an itinerary, but I want to have my own plan in place. I can't wait for the food, the parties, the culture, the history, and most importantly a chance for more readers to see my work. It feels like I'm finally moving forward in my career. I'm not sure how I got so lucky, but I earned it, and no one can take that away from me.

Chapter Twelve

I'm just getting out of the shower when my phone rings. I'm surprised to see Chelsie's number on the screen. I immediately get a strange feeling, like something big is about to go down. For some reason Bre pops into my head. I hope she's okay.

"I'm sorry it's so early," Chelsie says as soon as I answer.

"No problem. What's up?"

"There's actually something I need to talk to you about. Can you come to my office as soon as you get here?"

All of a sudden, a knot forms in my stomach.

"Sure. Is everything okay?" I ask nervously.

"Um, yes," she hesitates.

Crap. That wasn't convincing at all.

"Okay, I'll see you soon."

As soon as I'm off the phone, I rush to get ready. A million different thoughts begin to race through my mind. Chelsie would've told me if something was really wrong, right? I'm probably freaking out over nothing. I take a few deep breaths and prepare for my day, whatever it might bring.

As soon as I get to work, I make a beeline for Chelsie's office. When I walk in I pause at the door because she's not alone. There are three other people with her, including Aiden, our editor Kate Smith, and someone I don't recognize. Aiden gives me a worried look.

This isn't good.

"Thanks for coming so quickly, Erin," Chelsie says. "Please have a seat."

She points to the remaining empty chair in the office. I sit down on the edge, holding my coffee tightly in my lap.

"Erin, this is Laura Evans from HR," she says, pointing to the mystery woman in the room. "We've asked you to come in regarding the project you've been selected for." She's obviously been advised how to act and what to say. This doesn't sound like the Chelsie I know at all. "It's been brought to our attention that you and Mr. Thomas are romantically involved. This, of course, poses a problem, considering he was on the interview panel."

I don't say a word, and Aiden also remains silent, staring at the floor. This is exactly what he was trying to avoid.

Laura Evans speaks up. "Normally we don't have any policies or rules about staff members being involved, but with this situation it could be considered a conflict of interest.

Regardless, it complicates things, and we're waiting for Ms. Bufont to advise us how to proceed."

Okay, deep breaths Erin. We knew this was a possibility—but Aiden and I remained discreet in the office. Which can only mean one thing—someone complained about our relationship to cause issues.

"I'd like to add something," Aiden interjects. "Any kind of relationship we have outside of *Strike a Pose* in no way influenced my vote on the four individuals who were chosen to go the *Bleu Amour*. Erin earned her spot fairly, and everyone on the panel agreed that her submission was fantastic. Our responsibility as a group was to select the best candidates for this project—which is exactly what we did."

I give him a grateful smile, but I definitely hold back. I certainly don't want to show too much emotion in front of everyone.

"I have to agree," Kate Smith says. "I was on the panel, and Aiden didn't show any favoritism to Ms. Taylor."

Hah, this is our editor talking. They have to listen to her, right? Too bad she's not making the final call.

Laura types something on her phone. Working in HR is probably very difficult, I could never do it.

"As I said, we're waiting for Ms. Bufont to respond since this is a *Bleu Amour* managed project," she says finally looking up. "I can assure you this will not affect your employment here at *Strike a Pose*, Ms. Taylor."

I notice Aiden's shoulders relax a little as she continues talking.

"That being said, it could affect your position with *Bleu Amour.*"

My heart sinks. I knew it was too good to be true.

I clear my throat. "I understand. I just hope my work and time I've given to this magazine is taken into consideration." I sit up straight in my chair, holding my head up high. It's taking all my strength to keep it together and not burst into tears.

Laura nods her head. "Absolutely, that's why there's no question about your position here."

She holds out her hand to shake mine and then leaves the room after saying good-bye.

Kate Smith follows behind her, leaving me, Chelsie, and Aiden.

I want so badly to cry, but it's not the time or the place.

"Um, I actually need to run an errand," Chelsie says quickly. "You can use my office to collect your thoughts."

She grabs her bag and stops to pat me on the shoulder before she leaves. Aiden is still staring at the floor.

He probably feels terrible—but it's not his fault.

"I'm so sorry, Erin," he says, moving over to the empty chair next to me. "I should've asked to be removed from the panel as soon as things started to become more serious between us."

My stomach is completely twisted in a knot, and a lump has formed in my throat. I don't want him to feel like this all falls on his shoulders. Maybe I shouldn't have interviewed knowing he was on the panel. Regardless, something about this isn't sitting well, and I keep recalling Aly's sneaky comments about us owing Aiden.

"Please don't blame yourself," I say, clearing my throat. "We both knew this could be an issue. I guess I was naïve to think that because you only had one vote it wouldn't matter. And maybe it didn't until *someone* made a fuss—after the announcement was made.

Aiden gives me a curious look.

"So you're thinking someone raised concerns after you were selected?" he asks. "Do you really think one of your friends would actually do that to you?"

That's the big question here. If this was done to me on purpose, I'd hardly call them friends.

"Aly," I say flatly. "It has to be her."

Aiden looks completely shocked.

"I don't think so, especially after all the help you've given her.

"Don't underestimate her," I tell him, thinking about what Will said. "I'm starting to think her innocent act is just that, an act."

"Maybe," he says sounding unconvinced. "But she'd have nothing to gain from doing this to you. She was selected too."

"I know, but she's been making a lot of comments specifically about you and the interviews. Maybe she wants to be the one to shine, so she's pulling out all the stops to minimize her competition."

He twists his mouth to the side. Clearly he doesn't agree with my hypothesis, which is really frustrating to me.

"I see your point, but I just don't think she'd intentionally do anything to hurt you," he replies.

Both of us become silent, not looking at each other. I guess we're having our first disagreement.

"I suppose we'll just have to agree to disagree," I snap. I quickly stand up and move toward the door.

Aiden rushes behind me and grabs my arm to stop me. "Wait. Are you mad at me?"

I shake my head, not looking at him. "I just need a few minutes to clear my head. I woke up thinking I was going to Paris, and now it's looking pretty grim."

"Hang on." He puts his hands on my shoulders. "I know you're upset, but promise me you won't jump to any conclusions yet. This will all get worked out. I'm sure of it."

I bite my lip. "Okay. I'll try."

I open the door and head to my desk as I try to wrap my head around what just happened. I hate leaving Aiden like this, but it's really bothering me that he didn't back me up.

Both Bre and Aly are at their desks. Of course, they have their backs to one another. Sigh—just another fun day at the office.

"Bre, did you get my messages?" I ask.

"Yeah, I just wasn't ready to talk." She doesn't seem as upset as I thought she'd be, and I'm actually surprised she showed up today. I expected her to call in sick for a few days at least.

"Are you okay?" I ask cautiously.

"I'm all right. Luckily, I had *Harry* to help cheer me up." She practically yells Harry's name, which is silly because it's obvious Aly lost interest in him a while ago.

"That's good," I say. I sit down in my chair and put my face in my hands. The distraction of seeing Bre wears off quickly, and I'm reminded there's a very good chance I've lost my place on the project and possibly put my career in jeopardy. Laura from HR said my job is safe—but these situations can follow you.

I have nothing to say to Aly because I'm pretty sure she has something to do with this. I let out a frustrated sigh.

"What's wrong with you?" Bre asks curiously. "You look like someone kicked your dog."

Clearly I'm not good at hiding my disappointment.

"It's nothing," I lie. "Just tired."

Aly hasn't said a word since I got here. Is she feeling guilty? All that fake nonsense about me being a good friend to her and helping her when she started at *Strike a Pose*. I guess none of it was sincere—kudos to Bre for being right.

My phone starts buzzing from inside my bag, and when I take it out there's a text from Aiden waiting for me.

I'm so sorry. Please don't be mad at me.

I stare at the text. I'm not mad, more frustrated that he was so insistent of Aly's innocence. Maybe he likes all the attention she gives him? She doesn't exactly hide her crush. I put my phone back in my bag without responding to him. I just need time to sit with my thoughts and figure out what to do next.

"Erin, are you sure you're okay?" Aly asks a few minutes later.

When I turn around, I notice that she has a very concerned look on her face. I glare at her. *Stay calm.*

"I'm fine," I say, inhaling deeply. Unfortunately, my conversation with Aiden keeps replaying in my head. I know there's a chance I'm jumping to conclusions, but I can't shake the feeling that *someone* would betray me like this. "I guess I'm feeling a little overwhelmed about everything," I say with a frown.

She nods. "I understand. As exciting as it is, we're still leaving the country for two months. There's a lot to think about. She starts to ramble on about all the research she's doing and downloading apps to help her learn French quickly, and I zone out.

I'm growing more confused than ever.

I decide to pull a page out of Bre's book and leave the office early in hopes of avoiding Aiden and everyone else. There's nothing else I can do except patiently wait until my fate is decided.

As I drive home I play it over and over in my head. Maybe I'm completely overreacting. What if Aiden is right about Aly? For all I know it could have been Bre. Maybe she was mad because she wasn't selected.

I'd hope she wouldn't do that to me, especially because she had a hand in Aiden and I getting together in the first place. She may be a difficult person to work with, but she's not vindictive. At least I don't think so.

Ugh. What a mess.

And to make things worse, I hate the way my conversation with Aiden ended. Things have been going so good for us—and somehow our first disagreement is about Aly.

When I get home from the office, I heat up some vegetarian lasagna and pour a glass of wine. I reach for my phone and stare at the screen for a few minutes. I send Aiden a text.

I'm sorry about earlier. I overreacted.

As I pick at my food, I think about what my next steps should be. For starters, I'm going to meet with Chelsie in the morning and get her advice on how I could fight for the position I earned. One thing I know for sure is the panel was obviously impressed with my work, so hopefully that's enough. I don't know much about Madeline Bufont, but I've heard she's extremely particular when it comes to her staff. She has specific rules about food in the office and shoes her staff can wear. This is what worries me—she'd probably never tolerate a relationship in the office. And even though Aiden isn't coming to Paris, he had a hand in the selection process. Ugh. I wish I could shake the heavy feeling that's looming over me. If only I had a time machine, I'd do a lot of things differently.

I arrive at work bright and early yet again. Late last night, I sent Chelsie a message explaining that I desperately needed to talk to her. She responded and told me to be in her office first thing, so here I am. Ever since yesterday, I feel like everything is falling apart around me, and I can't sit by without trying to do something.

"Thanks for meeting with me," I say after she hands me a cup of coffee. Chelsie has the good stuff in her office. She has a fancy press thing that probably costs a fortune—anyway, it makes the best coffee, which is better than our cheap generic coffee pot in our lounge.

"Of course," she says. "How are you feeling?"

I sigh. "I've been better."

There are hundreds of thoughts swirling through my mind right now, but I need to stay focused on the reason I'm here.

"I'm just trying to figure out if there's anything I can do at this point. I know the final decision rests with Madeline Bufont, but do you have any suggestions?" I plead.

She shakes her head. "Unfortunately, I don't. It's completely out of my hands." She leans back in her chair. "I know this is difficult for you, but try not to worry too much. The panel as a whole selected you because of your submission. You're one of our most talented journalists, and there's no disputing that."

I force a smile. "Thank you."

She nods. "If there's anything I've learned in this career, it's to stay focused on the end game. Keep your head up, Erin. I see big things in your future."

I stand up and make my way to the door. Before I leave, I stop. "Chelsie, did Laura from HR tell you who made the complaint?"

She shakes her head. "No—do you have any suspicions?"

I frown. "I'm not positive. But I have an idea."

I thank Chelsie again and make my way back to my desk.

As soon as I sit down, I stare at my closed laptop. I need to do something productive instead of stressing about things that are completely out of my control.

Aiden hasn't responded to my text from last night yet. As much as I want to talk to him, seeking him out isn't in my best interest right now. Paranoia is setting in, and it almost feels like the walls have eyes. I'm not sure what to do next, so I open my laptop and start scrolling through emails—looking busy is probably the safest option right now. Of course I'm still curious about who went to HR, but I'll deal with that later.

"I need to talk to you," Bre whispers as soon as she arrives.

Seriously? It's almost lunchtime. Judging by her dewy and bright complexion, my guess is that she was at the spa or she's using some fabulous skin care products that I have to try.

"Okay," I whisper back. Now I'm whispering, too. Why does that happen?

"Later," she mouths, motioning toward Aly's desk, and Aly isn't even here.

Bre is acting strange, even more so than normal. I watch as she places two pictures of her and Harry on the desk. I'm assuming things are heating up between them. I guess the timing is right because she hasn't mentioned anything about not getting selected for the project. Perhaps finding her dream man outweighs living in Paris for two months.

Does this mean she's fired the dating doctor? I have so many questions.

After a few minutes I decide to send Aiden another text.

Can we talk tonight?

A few minutes later, he finally texts me back.

I think we need to. Meet in the lobby after work.

Ugh. His response causes a knot to form in the pit of my stomach. Between waiting for an answer about the project and my impending meet up with Aiden, my productivity is completely zapped. I spend the rest of the day watching YouTube videos on how to braid hair. I guess I can call this research if I ever decide to do a piece on hairstyles, which will never happen.

Bre disappears at some point during the day. I guess she didn't have to talk to me that urgently.

I wait until everyone in my department leaves, just in case I'm being watched and head down to the lobby a little after five. I know I'm probably overthinking it, but better safe than sorry right now.

Aiden is already there. He's sitting on one of the couches, looking at his phone.

"Hey, stranger," I say cheerfully.

"Hey."

Wow, that sure was a chilly greeting. I know our last conversation wasn't one of our finest moments, but I didn't expect him to be this cold. He stands up and heads toward the doors. I follow right behind him even though it feels like he's hundreds of miles away.

As soon as we turn the corner, I bring up our last conversation.

"Aiden, I want to apologize about yesterday. I totally overreacted, and I'm really sorry." I put my hand on his arm, and he looks at it as if it's poisonous.

He doesn't say anything for a few seconds.

"Who's Will?"

I open my mouth to say something, but nothing comes out. Why is he asking about Will?

"What?" I say absently.

"Will?" he spits out his name.

I'm so confused.

"Why do you ask?" I reply defensively. "He's a friend. A family friend, actually."

He gives me a questioning look. "Only a friend?"

Hold on. Why is he acting this way? When I mentioned Will to him, he barely paid any attention.

"I told you about him," I exclaim, an edge in my voice. "Don't you remember? I told you how my mom had this crazy idea of setting me up with her friend's son."

He throws his hands up.

"Erin, that was a while ago, before you and I started getting more serious. I didn't think you'd still be seeing him."

My mouth drops open in shock.

"Whoa. I'm not *seeing* him."

"Weren't you just with him the other day?" he asks.

What the hell? All of a sudden I remember running into Aly while I was with Will. Holy crap, she told Aiden that she saw us together.

"Ahh, let me guess. You talked to Aly," I exclaim. "Not that I'm surprised. Of course she had to tell you that she saw me with Will."

"Don't make this about Aly and the issues you two are having. This is about you and me."

"Are you serious right now?" I ask, raising my voice. "This is absolutely about Aly. Will and I are only friends. We met for coffee and ran into Aly and her friend. I can only imagine the version of the story she gave you."

Aiden and I are standing in the middle of the sidewalk facing each other.

It's a chilly San Francisco evening, and the air is even colder between Aiden and me. I refuse to give in and apologize when I've done nothing wrong.

"Aiden, I promise there's nothing going on between Will and me, but why do I feel like you already have your mind made up? Clearly you don't see Aly for the person she really is."

Aiden looks me in the eyes for the first time during our argument. He's breathing heavily, and I can tell by his frustrated expression that he wants to say something.

Of course I want him to say he believes me and not her. And

more than anything, I want to go back to that night we were together on my couch, talking and kissing.

"Aly didn't file the complaint with HR," he says calmly. "I asked her, and she insisted that she'd never do something like that. She knows how important this project is to you."

Wow, she definitely has him fooled.

"Maybe she didn't go to HR, but she doesn't care about me," I say sternly. "She took the first opportunity she had to tell you about seeing me with Will." It's taking all my strength to keep it together, but inside, I'm falling apart.

He doesn't respond and looks away.

"Well, I guess there's nothing more for us to say." I turn and walk briskly down the sidewalk, leaving him standing alone. I hear him call my name, but I keep walking and don't turn back.

Chapter Thirteen

$\mathcal{M}$y life is a mess right now. The day after my argument with Aiden I decide to pull a Bre and take a mental health day. I can't remember the last time I called in sick, so I'm definitely overdue. Although I don't go to the spa, shopping, or brunch like Bre would. I haven't left my couch, and I'm busy binging on the newest material Netflix has to offer. I know I'll have to face my fate eventually, but for now curling up under a blanket is exactly what I need.

When my phone rings, I cautiously look to see who's calling, and thankfully it's Mia.

"Hello," I say glumly.

"What the hell is happening out there? Do I have to come to the west coast to fix your life for you?" she shouts. I pull the phone away from my ear because she's so loud.

Tears begin to fall down my cheeks. When I can finally speak, I explain the details of my fight with Aiden through my sobs.

"Wait, who is Aly?" she interrupts. "Never mind, I'm booking a flight right now."

I have no doubt she's already online searching for plane tickets. At this point, I think she'd do more harm than good.

"No, you're not," I say calmly. There's nothing you can do right now."

"You know this is to be expected," she exclaims.

"What do you mean?"

"Come on. Aiden obviously got jealous when he heard you were hanging out with Will, and he's completely flipped out. That should tell you something."

"I don't know," I wail.

She laughs. "Clearly he can't deal with how strong his feelings are, so he reacted in the worst possible way."

"Maybe," I say, letting out an exasperated sigh. I'm too emotionally exhausted to dig into the concept of men and their issues with feelings.

"You know I'm right," she says. "Just promise me that you won't give up on him yet."

"I can't make any promises," I say.

"Sure you can," She insists.

Ugh, most of the time I appreciate Mia's positivity. But today it's kind of annoying. I lost count of how many life coaches and motivational conferences she's attended.

"So, what are we going to do about Paris?" she continues.

I groan. "There's nothing to do because I'm not sure if I'm going."

The rest of our conversation is all about Paris and the project. She suggests I put together a PowerPoint presentation to plead my case. Typical Mia, always the problem solver. Honestly, I'm just exhausted by the whole situation. All the joy and excitement of being selected has been sucked out.

After we get off the phone, I immediately get a text from my mother reminding me of our family dinner tomorrow night. As if things couldn't get any worse. I try to tell her I'm not feeling well, and she shows her usual concern in her response.

Take a vitamin C, and dinner is at 6.

Figures. I huff and puff as I respond to her.

Thanks for your concern, Mother.

As I'm getting ready for bed, I suddenly get the urge to call Aiden. The more I think about it, I want to try to fix things. What if Mia's right? What if he can't deal with his feelings, and that's why he had such a strong reaction when he heard about Will. I lay in bed for a while before I fall asleep. I have to put my life back together. If I want to go to Paris, I need to fight for it, and if I want to be with Aiden, I need to fight for him. I can't let anyone get in the way of my future.

"Aunt Ewin, let's play pwincess again," Kylie whines. I've been playing princess with Kylie since I arrived at my mother's, and I'm fine with it because I'd rather play with the kids all night than deal with the adults in my family.

"I promise we'll play princess after dinner," I tell her.

I remain mostly quiet as we all sit down at my mother's large dining room table. I wonder if she's one of the few remaining people in the world who uses a formal dining room.

I continue to pick at my food while my brother tells another boring story about one of his recent cases. Thankfully the subject of my life hasn't come up, so I suppose listening to Eric is better than that.

After dinner, I'm helping my mother clean up when she leans against the counter and gives me a curious look.

"What's wrong, Erin?" she asks. "You've barely said a word all night."

I place a bowl in the cabinet and drop my head. Before I know what's happening, a tear rolls down my cheek. I try to stop it, but that one tear opens the flood gates. I can't remember the last time I felt so vulnerable in front of my mother. Let's just say it's been a very long time.

"What is it?" she exclaims, putting her arm around me. She leads me to the table, and before I know it, I tell her everything. It's an explosion of ugly tears and profanity.

"Hey, Mom..." Eric interrupts. He stops in his tracks as soon as he sees me. "Oh, sorry."

My mom waves him out of the room and continues to rub my back.

"I don't understand why you didn't tell me about Aiden. I would've never pushed so hard for you to see Will had I known you already had a man in your life."

Crap. I'm not sure I really want to venture down the rabbit hole of our complicated relationship. We're actually having a mother-daughter bonding moment, and I don't know if I want to ruin it. I put my face in my hands.

"Erin?" she demands.

I exhale deeply. "What do you want me to say, Mom?" The tears begin to flow faster again. "Do you want me to tell you how much it frustrates me that you're constantly making me feel bad about my life? Do you want me to tell you that I'm tired of all the setups and blind dates? I've asked you numerous times to stop, and you don't."

Her eyes grow wide, and she looks slightly hurt by my outburst. She can't possibly tell me she didn't know how I felt.

"You're my only daughter," she exclaims. "I have every right to be concerned about your future."

I throw my head back in frustration. Is she even listening to a word I'm saying?

"Okay, Mom." The best thing I can do right now is just let it go because I'm too exhausted to continue hashing it out. I think it's time for me to go home.

It's been two days since everything fell apart. I'm sitting in Chelsie's office, waiting for Laura from HR to arrive. Apparently, a decision has been made about whether or not I'll be spending two months at *Bleu Amour*. I tried to get some information out of Chelsie, but she's not saying a word.

"None of this even matters anyway," I tell her. "Aiden and I aren't even speaking right now."

We're interrupted by Laura rushing into the office. "I'm sorry I'm late. Today isn't my day. There are fires popping up everywhere." She continues to ramble on while my future is hanging on by a thread.

I know that's a little overdramatic, but it is what it is.

Chelsie clears her throat. "Laura, I have a packed schedule today. Can we get to this matter, please?" She points at me, and I nod my head.

"Of course," she says with a chuckle.

Hah. I'm so glad she finds this funny while I'm sitting here sweating.

"I spoke with Ms. Bufont this morning. I'm afraid she feels that rescinding the offer is the only solution for this particular project. Now this being said, she feels your work is exemplary and she's open to you being a part of future projects. Unfortunately your relationship—"

"Aiden and I are no longer involved," I interrupt. Saying it out loud makes me feel sick to my stomach.

Laura continues, "I understand. However, Ms. Bufont runs a tight ship at *Bleu Amour,* and she'd rather not bring in any unnecessary tensions or issues into the mix. But as I said the other day, you're still a very valuable member of this team."

"Yes, you are." Chelsie chimes in.

Don't cry, don't cry, don't cry.

I swallow hard. "I understand."

I rise to my feet because I don't have the energy to argue. The decision has been made, and trying to fight it might only cause more problems. Before I leave, I hear Chelsie ask if they've selected someone to go in my place. Laura tells her they haven't decided if they will fill my spot. I hold my head up high and return to my desk. Truthfully, I'm not surprised. For some reason I never felt like this opportunity was really mine. I guess some things really aren't meant to be.

"There you are," Bre exclaims. "I can't remember the last time you didn't come into the office."

"I haven't been feeling well," I reply. This isn't a lie because I have been sick—sick to my stomach. Aly gets up and walks toward the elevator, completely ignoring us. She's probably mad because Aiden told her that I accused her of filing the complaint about us. Who knows if she's actually the culprit? I honestly don't know anything anymore.

"It looks like things are moving along well with Harry," I say, pointing to the pictures on Bre's desk.

She smiles. "Yes, except he's been traveling a lot. We haven't been able to spend much time together."

I nod. "Figures. That's what big corporate moguls do."

A look of shock spreads across her face. "You knew about Harry's career? Why didn't you tell me?"

I rub my temples vigorously. "Because it wasn't my place to tell."

She gives me a strange look. "I suppose. Anyway, what's happening with Aiden? I haven't seen him around in a few days."

I'm surprised she doesn't know. Bre is usually the first to know the office gossip. I assumed enough people were talking about it by now. Not to mention she has framed pictures of his brother all over her desk.

"Nothing is happening with Aiden," I say nonchalantly. "It just didn't work out between us."

Bre looks shocked. "What are you talking about? You and Aiden are meant for each other, so you just need to get over whatever your issues are."

My issues?

Bre's phone rings, and she immediately rushes out of the office as she answers it. I can't believe she's lecturing me about relationship drama. She's the one who hired a dating doctor. And considering how self-involved Bre is, I'm surprised she's so interested in my life. Ugh. I can't do this. Maybe I should just head home early.

As the afternoon continues, I'm unable to concentrate, so I head to the restroom to try to clear my head. When I see my reflection in the mirror, I cringe. I can't remember the last time I felt so overwhelmed. Between the news of not going to Paris and my fight with Aiden, it seems like everything is crashing down around me.

Aiden and I weren't even together that long. So why is this so hard for me? I sit on the counter in the restroom while I try to gather my thoughts. I have to turn this around. I just don't know how.

After what feels like hours, Kimmy walks in and sees me sitting on the counter. She gives me a funny look.

"I was just taking a few minutes alone," I tell her. "I woke up with a massive headache this morning."

She nods and moves toward me, leaning on the counter.

"I'm sure you're in shock," she says. "I don't understand how Bre always finds a way to come out on top."

I have no idea what she's talking about.

"What did she do now?" I ask.

Her eyes grow wide. "Didn't you hear? Bre's going to Paris."

Am I hallucinating, or did she just say Bre's going to Paris? How? Or—wait. This can only mean one thing. Bre is going to Paris instead of me...

"Erin?" Kimmy asks, waving her hand in front of me.

"Sorry. I'm just trying to make sense of all of this," I tell her.

She pats my arm. "I'm sorry. I'm sure this is difficult, and I'm not making it better. I just can't believe Bre is going—she doesn't exactly put forth as much effort as the rest of us. It really makes me question things."

Seriously, will she ever stop talking?

"I know what you mean."

She heads for the door but pauses before she walks out. "You know, at first I was upset when I didn't get selected, but I think there's a reason for everything. It may not seem like it now, but it's going to be okay." She gives me a half smile and leaves.

Wow. Is this really happening? Was Bre the one who filed a complaint about Aiden and me? But why? She's been one of our biggest cheerleaders.

And if this is true, then Aiden was right about Aly. Ugh, I need to fix things, at least with Aiden. My heart is racing, and my hands start to shake as I reach for my phone.

I'm not going to Paris. Can we talk soon?

It may be too late for us, but I hate leaving things the way they are. Aiden and I were friends before. Maybe we can at least get back to that point.

It's been two days since I got the news about not going to Paris. I'm sitting in the lobby of my favorite restaurant in Chinatown, waiting on Aiden. It took him almost a full twenty-four hours to respond to my text, but we agreed to meet for dinner to talk.

I've done an excellent job of avoiding both Bre and Aly over the last few days. Of course, you could cut the tension with a knife in the office. I feel bad for everyone else having to work with the three of us. I want more than anything to confront them both, but all in good time. Meanwhile my heart is racing, and my stomach is tangled in knots.

When Aiden walks through the door, it takes maybe half a second for all my feelings to rush back. I want more than anything to throw my arms around his neck, but I remain guarded, and he does the same.

"Hi," he says.

"Hi," I say softly. "Thanks for meeting me."

"Sure."

While we wait for the hostess to seat us, neither one of us speaks. I hate the silence, but I'm still trying to figure out how I want our conversation to go.

"So, you're not going to Paris?" he asks after we sit down.

I shake my head. "I guess it just wasn't meant to be."

He frowns. "I'm sorry, Erin. I wish I could go back and change things. I should've never been on that committee. I'm the reason you aren't going to Paris."

I know he feels badly, but this isn't his fault at all.

"Please don't say that," I insist. "I've had a lot of time to think about it, and I think deep down I knew I wouldn't be going."

"I'm sorry about everything that happened with Aly," he says, looking down at his hands.

I nervously chew on my lower lip.

"Aiden, my issue with Aly really didn't have anything to do with the job—it had to do with you. Every time she flirted with you, I got jealous...horribly jealous. Then, when I found out she told you about Will, I lost it."

Aiden listens intently, but he seems preoccupied.

"Maybe she didn't file the HR complaint about us, but she certainly went out of her way to come between us," I add. I'm about to ask him about Bre going to Paris, but he's not even looking at me. In fact, I seem to be doing most of the talking.

I reach across the table and take his hand. "Aiden, I promise you that there's nothing going on with Will. He really is just a friend."

Aiden grabs onto my hand and looks down.

"I have to tell you something," he says nervously. He doesn't let go of my hand, and I notice his grip tighten just a bit, making my heart race.

"Okay."

He takes a deep breath and starts talking, "That night, after our fight, some people from the office went out for drinks. I was really confused about everything, and I had one too many. More than I should've had. Aly showed up, and I told her about our fight." He pauses. "I was hurt and feeling sorry for myself..."

I'm starting to feel sick again. "And?"

"She kissed me..." he trails off.

I pull my hand back from his. This can't be happening. Maybe I'm imagining this. Or I'm dreaming, and I'm trapped in an episode of *General Hospital*. It takes all my strength to fight back the tears. I guess I was right all along. Aly wanted to make her move on Aiden—and she succeeded. The day she ran into Will and me played perfectly into her hands.

"Erin, please look at me," he pleads. "We were having a conversation, and it all happened so fast."

I make a face and shake my head. "So, she finally made her move on you. That's really classy of her to wait until you were incapacitated."

"I should've listened to you," he exclaims finally looking me in the eye. "I thought she was your friend, and I guess I fell for the sweet and innocent act. By the time I figured out what was happening, it was too late. I've felt awful since it happened, and I've been trying to figure out how to make it up to you. That's why I haven't reached out to you. I was so happy when you texted."

I feel dizzy. It all makes total sense, and I guess Bre was right about Aly all along.

"So, you say she kissed you? That's it, or did the kiss lead to more?" I ask coldly. "I'm assuming you kissed her back, but how much farther did you take it."

I don't know if I want to know the answer, but it's better to get it all out now so I can process it and move on.

"Nothing else happened," he exclaims. "She drove me home because there was no way I would've been able to make it. But I promise she dropped me off and didn't come inside my apartment."

I feel like I'm having an out-of-body experience. I'm sitting across from Aiden, listening to him tell me about making out with my alleged friend. I don't know what to say or do from here. Was he really *that* drunk, or was he trying to get back at me for going out with Will?

"Have you seen Aly since that night?" I ask.

"Only at the office," he insists. "I told her that what happened was a mistake and the only person I want to be with is you. I probably don't deserve your forgiveness because I didn't listen to you."

I want to forgive him more than anything. I want to forget this ever happened. But what I want more than anything is to go back to the moment we were together at my apartment when everything felt so perfect. Unfortunately, I don't have a time machine.

"I want to move on from all of this," I say softly. "I just need to think."

He nods. "And I believe you about Will. I completely overreacted, especially when we never agreed that we were exclusive. I...I messed everything up. Obviously you can be friends with whomever you want."

I watch his expression, and I can see that he's being sincere. Despite everything, I still want to be with him more than anything. But now I have to figure out if I can deal with all of this. Is there still a chance for us after what happened between him and Aly?

I barely touch my food, and after dinner Aiden and I walk outside. Neither of us says a word, and I shiver from the cold air.

"I hate how awkward things are between us," Aiden says, pulling me toward him. "I want to make this right, if you'll let me."

I nod. "I want that, too."

"I know you need time," he says. "And I'm going to give you that."

He kisses me on the forehead and walks away.

As I drive home, I try to put the puzzle pieces together. I guess after Harry rejected her, Aly decided to make a play for Aiden despite our involvement. I don't think she ever wanted to be my friend. The innocent newbie act was all a front, and I fell for it in the beginning too.

It's obvious that Aly does what she wants regardless of who it hurts. She wanted it all—to be a part of the Paris project and Aiden. And clearly nothing was going to stand in her way.

Chapter Fourteen

"Thanks for taking time out of your day to talk to me again," I tell Chelsie. I'm back in her office, and I'm on a mission. For the past few days, I've avoided Bre and Aly and have been concentrating on my writing. Inspiration has struck, and I'm working on an article that's going to wow everyone. This has been a long time coming, and in light of recent events, I think it may be the best work of my career thus far.

"I always have time for you," she says, sitting down with a cup of the world's best coffee.

I take a deep breath. Crap. I've been rehearsing what I wanted to say for the last few days, and now that I'm here I freeze.

Chelsie gives me a questioning look and starts talking before I have a chance to say anything.

"Erin, how have you been handling everything? I know how hard you've been working to further your career here.

Between you and me"—she lowers her voice—"I think their decision is absolutely ridiculous. Who cares if you and Aiden were dating? It was a group decision."

I give her a grateful smile, and she continues, "On that note, their loss is our gain. I certainly didn't want to lose you for all those months."

Talking to Chelsie makes me feel a lot better, and I know she has my back no matter what.

"I still wish I knew for sure who went to HR," I say. "I have a good idea but no definite proof."

She shrugs. "Erin, does it really matter? For all we know, it could've just been office gossip."

I shake my head. "I don't think so. I have a feeling someone did this on purpose. But you're right, it probably doesn't matter—and knowing wouldn't change anything."

"Did you and Aiden work things out?" she asks, conveniently changing the subject.

"No, and I'm not sure we'll be able to," I say sadly.

"That's a shame."

Just thinking about Aiden and that situation feels like a knife twisting in my chest.

"Anyway, I do have a very urgent request." I pause. "Can I move my desk? I know we spoke about it a while ago, but now it's completely necessary."

She smirks. "Are you asking for your own office again?"

I sigh. "That would be lovely, but right now I'd rather work in the restroom than where I'm currently sitting."

She laughs. "Well, you know the girls will be leaving for Paris soon. But let me get back to you. I may have a solution."

After my meeting with Cheslie, I'm feeling hopeful, something I haven't felt for a while. Right before I left her office, I gave her a hint about the piece I'm working on. In the meantime, I have to do some research.

I pull out my phone and call my sister-in-law.

"Hi, Liza, I need your help. When can you meet me?"

The next week practically flies by, probably because I've been putting in a lot of hours. I've realized that I completely lost sight of my goals and I have to get back on track. The team is heading to Paris in a few days, and I'm counting the minutes until they're gone—speaking of which, Aly and I completely ignore each other, and I'm fine with that. I had all these grand ideas about confronting her in front of everyone and calling her a dirty tramp, but I'm the better person.

Bre's bragging about Harry meeting her in Paris is extra annoying, but I try not to acknowledge it. I'm basically over the fact that she's going in my place, or at least I've come to accept it. We've never actually discussed it, but really, what would be the point? I'm busily pounding away on my laptop when Bre slides her chair over to mine.

"You should be going to Paris and not her," she says, pointing to Aly's desk. "We were working at this magazine when she was still in high school. It's ridiculous."

"It's fine," I reply, not looking away from my screen. "Although I still wish I knew who raised their concerns to HR."

Maybe something miraculous will happen and she'll admit that she was the one who sabotaged me. Or maybe she won't. I'm not expecting her to come clean if it was her.

"You really shouldn't be worried about that. You should be focusing on fixing your relationship."

I'm not surprised Bre would say that. It's always about men with her.

I roll my eyes. "You don't know the whole story, and frankly it's none of your business."

She pushes her chair back to her desk. "Fine. But you'll regret it. There's more to life than this job."

She will be gone soon. Just ignore her.

I don't leave the office until after dark, and it's freezing outside. When I get home, I put on my warmest pajamas and pour myself a glass of wine. As soon as I sit down on the couch with a blanket, I get a text from Aiden.

I miss you.

Ugh. Why does he have to torture me? I stare at my phone for a few minutes before responding.

I miss you, too. I wish things could be different.

Yeah, different as in I wish he never made out with Aly the second she threw herself at him.

~

Tomorrow is the big day, and I'm counting the minutes. The team is heading to Paris, and despite wanting to make a big countdown calendar for my desk, I decided that might be too obvious. I also don't need anyone accusing me of being jealous because I'm not.

My day starts out with an awkward elevator ride with Aly. I'm actually shocked when she speaks to me.

"Are you planning on ignoring me forever?" she asks.

"Was I ignoring you?" I ask, my voice dripping with sarcasm.

She glares at me. "Aiden told me that you think I'm the one who exposed your, um...relationship."

Why did I get on this elevator? I may have to use the stairs from now on.

"You couldn't be more wrong about me, and I'm hurt that you'd think I would stoop so low."

I shake my head as the door opens. I quickly push the button to close the door again and block her from leaving. As soon as the door closes, I turn to face her.

"You can't be serious," I say, folding my arms. "You'd never stoop so low? I would say kissing my boyfriend is pretty low."

She looks taken aback. "Oh, now he's your boyfriend? How many times did you say he *wasn't*? And you and Will are just *friends, right?*"

The elevator door opens again, and she slides past me.

"And let's be clear, I may have kissed Aiden first, but he certainly didn't stop me. You were the one who walked out on him."

What a piece of work Aly is. I feel so stupid for not seeing her true colors. Even self-involved Bre could see through her act. All the signs were there.

I snort. "Of course, he didn't stop you. He was drunk, and you took advantage of that."

"Sure. If that makes you feel better, go with that." She turns to walk away, but I stop her.

"And I'm not convinced you didn't go to HR about Aiden and me. I was so wrong about you, and someday this will all come back to bite you. You know what they say about karma."

"I already told Aiden I didn't do that," she says, raising her voice. "I'd never put anyone's job at risk."

I roll my eyes. "Right. You've made it pretty clear that you'll do whatever it takes to get what you want."

She sneers at me. "You started this by seeing someone behind his back. If you really liked Aiden, you wouldn't have gone out with Will."

This conversation isn't going anywhere, and I don't have to justify my friendships to anyone.

"Have fun in Paris," I say sarcastically. "I hope you can make it on your own."

As I walk away, I hear her say something else, but I don't stop. I've wasted enough time on her.

~

Strike a Pose is throwing a celebratory good-bye party for the Paris team for being selected for such an important project. At least that's what the invitation says. *Gag.* I shouldn't have to go to this good-bye party, right?

Yes, I'm having a bit of a pity party for myself this evening, but I'm still getting ready. It would look so much worse if I didn't attend. I'm a team player at *Strike a Pose,* and I'm going to show them that.

Tonight should at least be entertaining, and I've already had a glass of wine, so I'm starting to relax. After my altercation with Aly, I'm not looking forward to watching her prance around the event bragging about how hard she worked to make the team. Is it bad that I hope Bre shuts her up somehow? Normally I wouldn't be team Bre, but she's probably the lesser of two evils.

I'm sure Aiden will be there too. This will be the first time we'll all be in a room together since everything went down, so it's bound to be unbearably awkward.

I've gone out of my way to look my best tonight. My plan is to show up and act like I don't have a care in the world. I don't want anyone to think that I'm bothered about not going to Paris.

The party is at a local restaurant, and I'm a little surprised they're making such a big deal about it. Actually, not surprised...more annoyed. I take one more look in the full-length mirror in my room. Not too shabby in my little pink dress and Stuart Weitzman gold heels. I take one more sip of my wine and head out to catch a taxi.

Here goes nothing.

When I arrive at the restaurant, there's no sign of either Aiden or Aly. I head to the bar and order a glass of sparkling water.

"Erin, I'm so glad you're here," Kimmy squeals when she sees me. She takes a sip of the bright blue drink in her hand.

"Can you believe you and I have arrived before most of the team? I guess that shows they made the wrong decision, right?" She holds up her glass.

I force a smile.

"I think it shows how professional we are. We're being supportive of our coworkers."

"Whoa. I never thought of that. I like it." She pulls out a chair and sits down next to me.

"So, tell me what happened between you and Aly? I thought you and she were super close."

I hold out my glass to toast her. "Hmm...let's just say I was wrong about Aly. I gave her advice and was her friend when no one else gave her the time of day. She's not as sweet as she pretends to be."

"I think she's just really insecure," Kimmy says. "It's never easy being the new girl."

"And she kissed Aiden," I add.

Kimmy spits out some of her blue drink. "What? When?"

I tell her about what happened with Aiden and our fight. Kimmy and I have never really been close, but she's always been friendly, and I suppose we're bonding over our rejection now.

"So, are you and Aiden done?" she asks.

I shrug. "I don't know."

Kimmy and I are still talking when Aiden arrives. I watch as he walks through the restaurant, stopping to say hello to people. As soon as he sees me, he doesn't take his eyes off me. He moves quickly toward us, making my heart pound against the walls of my chest.

"I'll leave you two," Kimmy says loudly when she notices him. "See you later, Erin."

She walks away, leaving me and Aiden alone.

"Hey," he says.

"Hi."

This is so uncomfortable. I hate feeling like we're complete strangers.

"You look amazing," he says, eyeing my dress.

Hah, that's exactly what I was hoping he'd say.

"Thank you."

"I didn't think you'd be here tonight," he says, lowering his voice.

I give him a surprised look. "Why? Even though I'm not going to Paris, I want to show support for our magazine and the...team."

Well, everyone except Aly—and maybe Bre. Of course I don't say this out loud.

Speaking of Bre, she and Harry arrive at the party together, their hands linked. I guess they're official now. And they look like they just stepped off a runway. Bre in her tiny black dress and Harry in his tan suit and pale blue dress shirt.

"It looks like things are progressing for your brother and Bre," I say pointing toward the happy couple.

Aiden gives a shrug. "I guess. We'll see how long it lasts."

I'm not sure what he means by that, but I get the feeling that Aiden doesn't think it'll be long. We both grow quiet again.

"I should find Chelsie," I say, hopping off the bar stool. "I'll see you later."

Thoughts are racing through my mind as I make my way outside to the patio. Maybe I do need to move on from what happened between Aly and Aiden. He's told me how he feels, and I really miss him too. Why should I let Aly win? She's already going to Paris—I can't let her succeed in coming between Aiden and me.

I head back inside with plenty of built-up courage, ready to run straight back into Aiden's arms. Before I take two steps inside, someone calls my name.

"Erin?"

I turn around, and there's Will with his usual cheesy grin.

"Will? How are you?" I'm so surprised to see him that I forget what I was about to do.

"Doing good, buddy," he says, giving me a hug. He introduces me to his friends. Of course, I'll never remember their names. "What brings you here?" he asks.

I'm instantly reminded about my plan to talk to Aiden.

"Our magazine is throwing a send-off party for team that's heading to Paris."

"And you weren't going to say good-bye? I'm going to have to tell your mother," he teases.

My face falls, and Will's eyes grow wide. "Oh, I'm sorry. I just assumed you were going."

I wave my hand. "Please don't apologize. It just wasn't meant to be."

There's no way I'm getting into what happened with losing my place on the project.

I glance over at the bar and see Aly staring at me. Lovely. I'm sure she's plotting to run and tell Aiden about me talking to Will. I scan the room and find Aiden talking to his brother and Bre.

"What are you looking at?" Will asks. I turn back to him, and in frustration, I shake my head and exhale loudly.

"Do you remember Aly, the girl we ran into at lunch?"

He nods his head. "Yeah, you were asking me if I thought she was the devil."

198 • MELISSA BALDWIN

"Ha-ha," I reply. "Well, she *is* the devil, and she's about to wreak more havoc on my life once again."

I quickly explain what Aly's been up to, and he glances over at her. She's pretending to ignore us now, but I know she's been watching the whole time. She's shown that she'll do what she needs to in order to destroy any chance I have with Aiden.

Before I have time to react, Aiden starts coming towards us. Now is my chance to prove that Aly has been up to no good.

"Hey. I was looking for you." He eyes Will curiously and holds out his hand. "Aiden Thomas."

Will shakes his hand. "Hey. I'm Will."

I inhale sharply as I wait for what happens next. Aiden looks at me and back to Will.

"You're Will, as in the family friend Will?"

Will nods. "Yep, that's me. Small world running into Erin here," he says nonchalantly.

He looks at me and smiles. "Anyway, I better get back to my friends. Good seeing you again, Erin, and nice meeting you, Aiden."

He saunters away, leaving Aiden and me alone again. I look at him and hold my head up high.

"So that's Will?" he asks awkwardly.

"Yes, seeing him here was a coincidence. I was telling him about Par—"

"I told you, Aiden," Aly interrupts. "What are the chances that Will would show up here tonight?"

I'd really love to finally let loose and tell Aly what I really think, but this isn't the time or place. I hold my tongue and look at Aiden to see his reaction.

"Aly, this doesn't concern you," Aiden says not taking his eyes off me. He grabs my hand and leads me to the door, leaving Aly fuming behind us.

Chapter Fifteen

*A*s soon as we step out into the cold air, I start rambling.

"I really had no idea Will would be here tonight."

Without a word he pulls me toward him and kisses me hard. At first I don't move, and then it happens...I wrap my arms around his neck and kiss him back. We're right in front of the restaurant where anyone could see us, and I don't care. Not about Paris, or the big office, or Aly, or anyone. It's almost as if we're the only two people in this city, and I don't want this feeling to ever go away.

"I'm so sorry for everything," Aiden says when he finally pulls away. He clasps his hands around my waist. "It's all my fault. I should've told you how I was feeling. The day you told me about your mother setting you up with Will, I was dying inside, but I was afraid to say anything. I wasn't sure how you were feeling, and I didn't want to rush things."

I'm completely surprised by his admission. I can't believe he was bothered about Will. He acted so nonchalant when I told him.

"I should've told you that I went out with Will, even as friends," I tell him.

He shakes his head. "I should've never defended Aly. She really made it seem like you and her had grown close." He looks down at the ground. "I can't begin to tell you how sorry I am."

I take his face in my hands. "You were not the only one to be fooled by her. But I don't care anymore. She's leaving tomorrow, and it will be eight wonderful weeks without her or Bre."

We stand on the sidewalk talking and kissing. When it's time to go inside, he takes my hand.

"Are you sure you want to do this?" I ask.

"Absolutely. I'm done hiding my feelings for you." He kisses my hand and leads me back to the party.

I may not be going to Paris, but having Aiden by my side totally makes up for it.

Aly spends the rest of the night shooting me dirty looks and saying random words in French. I manage to steer clear of her until we run into each other in the bathroom, or maybe she followed me. She stands next to me in front of the mirror where I'm reapplying my lipstick. She takes out her makeup bag and leans against the counter.

"Doesn't it bother you that Aiden was kissing me just a few weeks ago?" she asks. She even makes a point of pursing her lips and makes kissing faces in the mirror. I see that her immaturity is finally starting to shine through amongst her many other undesirable qualities.

I stare straight ahead in the mirror and ignore her.

"You know you're always going to wonder if he really drank that much or if he just wanted to kiss me."

I'm not going to let her get to me.

"I don't think so," I say when I finally look at her. "I'm willing to put it behind us. Aiden has told me how much he cares for me, and I'm going to trust him."

Her smug smile fades.

"I'm actually glad I'm not going to Paris because I get to stay here with him." I turn to face her. "Anyway, good luck making it on your own at *Bleu Amour*. You certainly needed my help to get you there."

I walk out of the bathroom feeling like I'm on cloud nine.

When I return to Aiden, he wraps his arm around me and kisses me on the cheek. Harry starts clapping in our direction.

"It's about time you kids got it together," Harry announces. "I was starting to think my little brother had no game and more issues than I thought."

He laughs, and Aiden reaches over and hits the back of his head.

"I'm not the one with issues, bro," Aiden says with a laugh. "You're dating Bre. Best of luck with that one, you're going to need it."

I try to hide my giggle, and thankfully, Bre isn't around for this conversation. Although Harry doesn't seem phased by anything Aiden says about Bre. Maybe Aiden is wrong about them not lasting.

"Bre keeps life interesting," Harry says with a wicked grin.

"What do I do?" Bre asks, joining us. She raises her eyebrows when she sees Aiden's arms around me.

"Bre, can we talk for a minute," I say as I pry myself away from Aiden. I lead her over to an empty bar table.

"I just wanted to tell you that you were right all along about Aly."

The corner of her mouth curls up. "Ah, so you've finally seen the light. Took you long enough."

I roll my eyes. "I was trying to be nice and helpful to the new girl."

She gives me a smug look and takes a sip of her wine. "Whatever. Learned your lesson, didn't you?"

Unfortunately, she has a point.

"Yeah, I guess the fact that Aly took advantage of Aiden when he was drunk says it all."

Her mouth drops open. "What?"

"Yep."

She pretends to act shocked, but I'm sure she's gloating inside.

"Well, it sure seems like you're over it now," she says. I glance over at Aiden who flashes me one of his brilliant smiles.

"Yeah, I think everything is finally moving in the right direction. I guess it's good that I'm not going to Paris, after all. Maybe I should be grateful to the person who filed the HR complaint.

"Really?" Bre says, sounding surprised.

I can't believe I just said that, but being angry isn't going to change anything.

For the first time in a while, Bre isn't getting on my last nerve, but I'm dying to get back to Aiden. I think we've spent enough time apart.

"Anyway, have a wonderful time in Paris with Aly." I start to walk back to where Aiden is waiting for me.

"It was me, Erin," she calls.

I freeze and turn to face her. "What?"

She lets out a deep sigh. "It was me. I'm the one who complained to HR about you and Aiden. I was mad that they didn't choose me, and I—I'm really sorry."

I'm completely speechless. I had my suspicions, but I really didn't believe she would actually do something like this.

"What?" I snap.

I don't know how to respond to any of this. She seems to be sincerely sorry, well as sincere as Bre can be.

"You just said you were grateful because you get to stay here with Aiden."

I stare at her as if she's lost her mind. "You know I thought it was odd when you took my place, but I tried to put those suspicions out of my mind because we were supposed to be friends."

"I am your friend."

I snort. "Sure. You know I've always given you the benefit of the doubt even through all your nonsense. How could you do this to me?"

She looks down at the floor and doesn't say anything.

I shake my head in disgust and head toward the door. What the hell? In the last few days I've learned that two people I trusted aren't really my friends after all. One was out for my job and one for my man. As soon as I step outside, my eyes fill with tears.

"Erin, what's wrong?" Aiden asks, joining me.

I immediately run to him as the tears begin to fall. "I just want to go home."

I never thought I'd feel so sad cuddling with Aiden on my couch. I love the fact that he's here with me, but I'm just so disappointed after hearing Bre's admission. I know I shouldn't be surprised because this is Bre we're talking about. I guess there's a part of me that thought we were really friends.

Aiden insisted on driving me home from the party, and then he insisted on coming inside until I calmed down.

"So, are you going to offer me a drink? I've been thinking about Yoo-hoo since the last time I was here," he asks, his lips on the top of my head.

I know he's trying to cheer me up. "I'm sorry I'm being such a terrible host. Please help yourself."

He runs to my kitchen, and I pull the warm blanket tightly around my body. He returns with two Yoo-hoos and the package of Oreos. When he sits on the couch next to me, he pulls my legs onto his lap.

"I can't believe Bre did this to you. I'm telling Harry because he needs to know what kind of person she is," he says, taking a sip of his Yoo-hoo.

"I should've known," I say with a shrug. "The crazy thing is that she went on and on about what a terrible person Aly is. And then she does something like this."

Aiden pushes my hair out of my face and kisses my hand.

"It's hard to concentrate on my pity party when you do that," I tell him.

He gives me a mischievous smile. "Good. I don't want to waste any more time." He leans in and gently kisses me again.

This is exactly what I need to forget all about Bre and Aly.

"Isn't it a glorious day?" Kimmy sings as soon she walks in.

It's been two days since the Paris team left, and the office has been an absolute dream.

"Yes," I agree. "It's amazing how different it feels around here with um…fewer people."

She giggles.

"I actually wrote Chelsie an email telling her that I hope Aly and Bre stay in Paris forever, but I deleted it before sending."

"I love it," Kimmy exclaims. "You should've sent it."

I admit it felt good to type it out even though I didn't send it. I think that's some kind of therapy tactic, and it really does work.

Bre has tried to reach out to me several times, but I haven't responded. I have nothing to say to her.

More importantly, it's time for another Taylor family dinner, and I really want to bring Aiden. I know it would make my mom's year if I actually brought a man home, but I don't know if I'm ready for that. Aiden and I are in a good place, and I don't know if I'm ready to unleash the Taylors on him just yet. My brother has been known to rub people the wrong way on more than one occasion. And I'm afraid my mother will start planning our wedding before we even get to the dessert.

My mom answers right away when I call her.

"Hi, Mom."

"Please tell me you aren't calling to cancel out on dinner?"

"It's nice to talk to you, too, and no, I'm not calling to cancel." I pause. "I'm actually calling to ask if I can bring someone."

There's silence on the other end of the phone.

"Mom? Are you still there?"

"I'm here," she says. "Who do you want to bring? Is it Will? He's such a nice guy."

I can't disagree with her. Will is a great guy, but he's not Aiden.

"Sharon would be thrilled. I could invite her, too."

"Mom," I interrupt. "I'm not bringing Will. I've told you a million times that he and I are only friends."

"I know, I know." She huffs. "That doesn't mean he can't come to dinner though. You don't have to get so defensive?"

I'm trying to keep my cool, but she continues to push. I remind her of a few weeks ago when we had our brief fleeting moment of mother-daughter bonding time.

"Remember when I told you about Aiden?" I ask. "I started crying in the kitchen, and you actually comforted me."

Okay, that was a low blow. Thankfully, she doesn't catch on to my insult.

"Anyway, I was thinking of inviting him to dinner. *But* if I do, I have some guidelines we need to discuss."

"Is this the same man who you said was jealous of you and Will?" she asks.

I let out an exasperated sigh. "Mom, there is no *me and Will.*"

Sigh. I'm already regretting this conversation.

"Of course, I look forward to meeting Aiden," she exclaims. "And don't worry about guidelines. I know exactly how to handle myself."

Ugh. What have I done?

Chapter Sixteen

"*I*t's going to be fine. And I promise not to embarrass you in front of your family," Aiden says.

Ha. He has no idea what he's in for. I've tried my best to prepare him for my mother and my brother. Granted, I'm sure there are more dysfunctional families out there than mine.

We're on our way to my mother's house. She's called me several times in the last few days to find out what I'll be wearing and what Aiden's favorite foods are. I let the last eight calls go to voice mail and ignored her texts.

"And remember to just ignore my brother. He has the 'who's car is bigger' mentality when it comes to new people. He's arrogant and entitled, and don't feel guilty if you want to punch him before dinner even starts," I tell him.

Aiden grabs my hand and squeezes it. "Stop worrying. I got this."

Easy for him to say. Worrying comes naturally when dealing with my family. And Aiden is the first man I've felt this strongly about in a long time. I don't want anything or anyone else getting in our way.

When we pull up, I freeze. It's not too late to turn around and go home.

"Let's go, ET." Aiden gets out and comes to my door. He leads me out of the car and wraps his arms around my waist. "I promise I'm still going to like you when this dinner is over."

Ha-ha. We'll see.

"Come in, come in," Mom screams, before we even get to the door. She runs straight to Aiden and throws her arms around him. She's wearing an apron that says *Yes, I'm a grandma and I look this good!*

Ugh. I already need a drink.

"Aiden, I'm so happy you're here. Come with me. We can chat in the kitchen." She links her arm in his and drags him into the house.

"Hi to you, too, Mom," I say.

"Erin, honey, please hang up your coats," she calls over her shoulder. I roll my eyes as I throw our coats on the bench in the entry hall. I hurry to the kitchen where I find Aiden sitting on a barstool drinking a Coke. Really? I would've thought he needed something stronger already.

"You'll meet Eric and Liza and the kids soon. And Erin's father should be here any minute."

"Dad's coming to dinner?" I interrupt.

She looks at me as if I've lost my mind. "Of course, honey. It's a family dinner."

I already told Aiden about my parents' interesting relationship.

"Tell me all about your family, Aiden," she demands.

Aiden does exactly what she asks. I listen intently as he talks about his parents and Harry. When he mentions Harry, I cringe thinking about Bre. This causes a random thought to pop into my head. What if Harry and Bre continue their relationship? I may never escape her.

"We're here," a voice calls.

Eric walks in carrying baby Knox. He looks at Aiden and then at me and gives a curious smile.

Let the fun begin.

"Hey, man, Eric Taylor, and this is my son, Knox." He holds out his hand to Aiden.

Aiden nods. "I'm Aiden, Erin's boyfriend."

All of a sudden I get tingles all over my body. This is the first time he's referred to himself as my boyfriend out loud, and he says it to my brother.

"Erin's *boyfriend*," Eric says a wicked grin spreading across his face. Just then, Liza walks in with Kylie. She looks around the kitchen curiously.

"This is my wife, Liza, and Kylie," Eric introduces them proudly. "Liza, this is Erin's *boyfriend*, Aiden."

And so it begins.

"Aunt Ewin, let's play pwincess," Kylie yells as she starts pulling my hand.

Hell yeah, I'll play princess. Anything to get me out of this kitchen.

"What about you, Aiden?" I ask. "Would you like to play princess with us?"

He laughs. "Well, my crown is in the shop today, but sign me up for next time.

Next time? So far so good.

While Kylie and I play, I can hear my family and Aiden laughing in the kitchen, so I guess it's a good sign that he hasn't tried to sneak out yet.

After a while my dad pops his head into the playroom. "I met your new friend. He seems like a decent guy."

"Is he okay? I left him with Mom and Eric."

"He's still alive, and he's still here," he says, laughing. "I'd say the worst is over."

I leave Kylie happily playing on her own and rush to save Aiden.

"That's a great story," Aiden exclaims. He and Eric are laughing hysterically as if they've known each other for years.

"Hey, ET," Eric yells as soon as he sees me.

I shoot a dirty look at Aiden. Really? He had to tell my brother about the ET nickname.

"Sorry," Aiden mouths.

"I love this guy," Eric says to me. "What took you so long to bring him home?"

I raise my eyebrows. "You. I like him and didn't want you to scare him away."

Eric gives me a surprised look. "Why would I do that? I even like him better than Wilbur."

Crap.

"Who's Wilbur?" Aiden asks.

"Wilbur is my friend's son, family friends," my mom chimes in. "Dinner's ready."

Perfect timing. I can tell by his expression that Aiden has figured out that Will and Wilbur are the same person. I grab his hand. "Sorry I left you with them. You okay?"

"Yep. So has your whole family had the pleasure of meeting Will?"

I shift uncomfortably. "Yeah, remember I told you about that horribly awkward meeting at Kylie's party? That was Will. Mom and Sharon concocted a plan and forced Will to come to the party."

Aiden gives a shrug. "Well, it's over now. Let's enjoy the evening.

Easy for him to say.

He leads me toward the dining room.

We all sit down at the table, and Eric has obviously gone long enough without talking about himself. He starts in about a new boat he's looking at buying for Christmas. I actually don't mind him monopolizing the conversation because that means we aren't talking about me and my personal life.

Aiden has managed to make himself at home with my family, and dinner is going very smoothly until little Kylie makes an announcement.

"Grandma and Papa were kissing like a pwincess and pwince," she says as she takes a bite of her spaghetti.

The room goes silent, and we all stare at my parents. They both look like a couple of teenagers who've been busted for making out.

"Kylie," Liza scolds.

"They didn't see me." She giggles. "Grandma kept saying, 'Oh, Eddie.'" She pauses and looks at my mom. "Grandma, who's Eddie?"

My parents exchange glances.

"I guess we've been caught," my dad exclaims. "Let's just tell them, Margie."

She smiles and puts her hand on his cheek.

"We've decided to get remarried," he announces. "We've realized our divorce was premature, and we both needed to experience some companionship from other people to really appreciate each other."

I look at Aiden who's clearly enjoying every second of this.

"None of the other men out there compare to your father, and believe me, I've tried them," my mom exclaims.

I put my face in my hands, and Liza quickly excuses herself to take Kylie to the playroom to watch a movie.

"Mom, too much information," I announce, raising my voice.

She gives me a confused look. "I'm just being honest, honey. Anyway, your father and I are booking a family cruise, and we'll be married by the ship's captain. That being said, we'd like to pick a date tonight so we can get it booked. Aiden, I expect you'll be joining us, too."

Aiden's eyes grow wide, and he glances at me. "I'd love to go. Thanks for including me."

My head is spinning. In the last few minutes my parents are caught making out by my five-year-old niece, my mother talks about being with other men, my parents announce they're getting remarried, and Aiden has accepted an invitation to come on a family cruise.

"So, do you want to come on a cruise with me?" he asks, flashing me a warm smile.

I scoff. "Very funny. Shouldn't I be asking you that question?"

He shrugs his shoulders. "I've already been invited. I know better than to turn down an invitation from a bride-to-be."

"Aiden, I knew I liked you," my mom says, taking a sip of her wine.

Eric gets up, hugs our mom, and gives Dad a high five. "Excellent news. Erin, aren't you happy Mom and Dad are getting remarried?"

Why would he even ask me that?

"Of course," I snap. "I'm just taking it all in...the announcement, the cruise, everything. It's a lot." I glance at Aiden.

I'm still trying to wrap my head around Aiden joining my family on a cruise for my parents' second wedding. It all feels so surreal, but my family has never done anything simple.

After dinner, I pull Aiden away for a private moment before he joins Eric and my dad for a game of blackjack.

"Is everything okay?" he asks.

I nod. "I'm sorry about all this. I warned you that my mom could be a little much. Please don't feel obligated to come on this wedding cruise getaway, or whatever it is."

His face falls. "You don't want me to come?"

Whoa. Is he serious?

"Of course I want you there," I exclaim. "I just don't want you to feel obligated—you just met my family."

He takes my face in his hands. "I can't think of any place I'd rather be. Stop worrying." He leans in and firmly plants a kiss on my lips. "Can I go play cards with your brother now?"

I groan. "If you want to."

I sit down on the couch and pull my knees into my chest and look around at my crazy family. Okay, I guess they aren't that bad. Aiden's having a great time playing cards, my mom and Liza are looking through bridal magazines, and Kylie is watching *Frozen* for the millionth time. I guess Aiden does fit in well, maybe even better than me.

I'm completely exhausted after another enlightening Taylor family dinner. I quickly get ready for bed, and just as I'm about to drift off to sleep my phone rings.

"I got your message," Mia says as soon as I answer. I glance at the time. *Does this girl ever sleep?*

"Isn't it the middle night in Florida? And are you talking about my message from a few days ago?" I ask.

"I know, I know, but Jack had to take me to the Bahamas," she says with a sigh.

"Poor you. It must have been torturous."

"Miserable," she says with a giggle. "Anyway, give me the scoop."

I can barely keep my eyes open, so I give her the condensed version of what happened with Aly, Bre, and of course Aiden. As soon as I end the call, I get a text from Aiden.

Can't sleep. Miss you. Sweet dreams.

I don't think sweet dreams will be a problem for me tonight. Watching Aiden be so patient with my family made me like him even more than I already did. My feelings are growing stronger by the day, which makes me both excited and terrified.

I arrive at the office bright and early. It's amazing how different the energy is in without Bre and Aly here. I have a busy day planned that includes finishing up my article as well as putting together a business plan for my promotion. Granted, I haven't been offered a promotion, but I'm going to plead my case. I have nothing to lose, especially after I professionally and gracefully accepted their decision when they rescinded their offer to go to Paris.

"You've been busy," Kimmy says, looking over my shoulder. She's moved to Bre's desk, and it's nice to have a neighbor who's pleasant after so many years of Bre. We moved all of Bre's things to Kimmy's old desk.

"I'm really excited about this piece I've been working on. I think it's finally ready to send to Chelsie," I say, clasping my hands together.

"Well, are you planning on telling me about it? You've never been this secretive about your work."

She's right, but in light of recent situations, I'm a bit leery of my coworkers. Kimmy's never done anything to prove she isn't trustworthy, but better to be safe than sorry.

"It's not a secret—I'm just not ready to share it yet," I say. "But I promise you'll be one of the first to read it."

The word on the street is that the Paris team is doing very well, other than a few small issues. The best news I've heard is that Madeline Bufont had to put Aly in her place after she crossed some boundaries. Apparently, Aly now believes she's an expert on how to run a magazine, and she had the nerve to give Madeline a few pointers. I would have given my left arm to have witnessed that. Perhaps this will be her first and last chance to work with *Bleu Amour*. Karma has a funny way of coming back around.

I haven't heard anything specific about Bre, but she knows her limits. She'd never attempt to cross Madeline Bufont.

I'm so engrossed in my work that I don't notice Aiden watching me.

My face lights up when I see him. "Well, hello."

"Hi, gorgeous. I was wondering if you'd like to have lunch with me. Do you think your boyfriend will care?"

I make a face. "Hmm…he might get a little upset, but we don't have to tell him."

Everyone else has already left for lunch, so I grab my bag and link my arm with Aiden's. We head across the street to the café, and as soon as we're seated, Aiden speaks up.

"I have a request, ET. Saturday is my parents' anniversary dinner, and I was hoping you'd accompany me. And since you owe me after I endured a night with your family, you could return the favor."

I totally owe him, but I'm also excited that he wants me to meet his parents.

"I'd love to."

A relieved smile spreads across his face.

"I'm assuming Harry will be there?" I say. "Has he said anything about Bre?"

He rolls his eyes. "Unfortunately, yes. He told me she's devastated about what happened between you and her and she's planning to make it up to you. Blah, blah…" He pauses.

"Please don't let that keep you from the dinner. I want you there, by my side."

Ha. There's no way I'd let Bre keep me from meeting Aiden's parents.

"I'll be there."

"Excellent. Oh, and make sure you dress to impress because we're going to the French Laundry."

Wait. *What?* The French Laundry is one of the most exclusive and best restaurants in the entire world.

"Really?" I squeal. "I've always wanted to go there."

I guess I can forget a relaxed meeting with Aiden's parents. I'm going to be worried about using the wrong fork all night.

"ET, you look worried. What are you thinking about?"

I don't want to tell him that I'm stressing out about place settings.

"Not worried at all," I reply nonchalantly. "Just excited."

That's a total lie. I need Mia—I'm going to need help choosing an outfit and a crash course in fine dining etiquette.

"French Laundry? Are you freaking kidding me?" Mia exclaims. "It sounds like you've hit the jackpot, my friend."

"Ha, says the girl who's dating a Hemsworth brother who whisks her off to the Bahamas every other weekend."

She laughs, but she knows I'm right.

I tell Mia about the dilemma of Aiden's brother dating Bre. I have no idea if Bre has met their parents yet, and I know it shouldn't matter.

"The girl is on another continent, so you have nothing to worry about," Mia exclaims. "This is your chance to get to know Aiden's parents, and they're going to love you."

I appreciate her confidence in me.

"But what if they already love her?" I wail. "It doesn't sound like she and Harry are breaking up anytime soon. There's a very strong possibility I'll have to deal with Bre on a regular basis as long as we're dating brothers."

Mia lets out a huge sigh. I can tell she's getting frustrated with me.

"I know I'm being ridiculous, but I haven't felt this way about anyone in a long time. I don't want anything to mess it up." And there it is.

"Erin, are you saying what I think you're saying?"

Excitement fills my body as I'm ready to admit to my feelings.

"Yes, I think I'm falling in love with Aiden," I say, my voice barely above a whisper.

"Finally," she shouts. "It's about time you admit it, and now you can bring him on vacation to Florida."

Well, considering we're already going on a cruise together, I guess a trip to Florida isn't out of the question.

"We might be able to arrange that," I say with a laugh.

"That's the best news I've heard all year."

Chapter Seventeen

I feel like I'm going to throw up. Tonight's the night of Aiden's parents' anniversary dinner, and I'm a wreck. Not only is it my first time meeting them, but it also happens to be at one of the most exclusive restaurants in the entire world. I've taken about fifteen photos in different outfits and sent them to Mia. We finally decide on a form fitting black jumpsuit with a black Gucci belt and black stilettos.

Once my decision has been made, I sit down in front of the TV with a glass of wine to relax. I hear my phone buzzing, and it's a text from Aiden.

Can't wait to see you tonight. Be there at 5.

I'm a bit embarrassed to admit this, but I've been daydreaming all day about Aiden telling me he loves me. I know without a doubt how I feel about him, and I think he has strong feelings for me, but I'm not sure to what extent. He definitely passed the family test. After our dinner, my mom called me gushing nonstop about how great Aiden is. The only thing that got her off the subject of him was her impending nuptials. I still can't believe my parents are getting remarried, but then again, I'm still not over the fact they got divorced in the first place.

Aiden arrives promptly at five o'clock, and we don't waste any time. I'm so anxious on the way to the restaurant, I can barely sit still. When we pull up at the restaurant, I check my makeup in the mirror for the tenth time. Out of the corner of my eye, I catch Aiden watching me.

"What?" I ask him.

He shrugs. "Just looking at you. And by the way, have I told you how stunning you look tonight?"

I giggle. "Only about twenty times."

"Well, make it twenty-one." He leans over and kisses me softly. I wrap my arms around his neck, but I quickly drop my arms.

"We can't do this now," I say, pointing at the restaurant.

"Let's skip dinner," he suggests, pulling me close to him again. He smells so good—clean and masculine.

I'm tempted to agree, but I'm dying to eat at French Laundry and of course meet his parents.

"We can't."

Aiden huffs and puffs as he opens the door and moves to my side of the car.

When we get inside, Harry is already there with their parents.

"Hello, ET," he says playfully.

I force a smile. "Hello, Harrison."

He makes a face. I guess he doesn't love being called by his full name. I have no doubt that the only time he's referred to by his full name is when he's in trouble.

Aiden takes my hand and introduces his parents.

"It's lovely to meet you, Erin. We're glad you could join us," Mr. Thomas says.

"Thank you for having me, and happy anniversary."

They're both very polite and formal. I'm not sure if this is how they always are or if it's just our dinner location.

Aiden's mother fixes her husband's and sons' collars. She's so graceful, and I can see how much the men in her life adore her.

Once we're seated, I begin to relax a bit. Everything is going smoothly up until Harry opens his big mouth and mentions his upcoming travel plans.

"I'm heading to Paris in a few days to see Bre." He glances at me. I give a slight nod and take a sip of my water. I wonder if he's trying to provoke me.

"How wonderful. When are we going to meet this mystery girl of yours?" Mrs. Thomas asks. Ah, so they haven't met Bre yet.

"Very soon, Mother. She'll be back in a few weeks, and I have a feeling you'll really like her."

Aiden reaches over and puts his hand on my leg. I give him a grateful smile. I'm not going to say a word about Bre. Tonight is about making a good impression and getting to know Aiden's family, and my feelings about Harry's girlfriend really don't matter.

"Aiden told me you all work together at the magazine," Mrs. Thomas says. Thankfully Aiden jumps in before I have a chance to say anything about Bre.

"Yes, Mother," he says. "Bre is working on location in Paris for a few months."

His mother looks impressed. "That's exciting. She must be very talented if they sent her to Paris. Have you been to Paris, Erin?"

Aiden shoots an apologetic glance in my direction.

I force a smile. "Not yet. Hopefully one day."

She grins and gives a nod. A few seconds later I decide to visit the restroom.

As I stand up, I almost trip over the long tablecloth. Thankfully I catch myself from a potentially humiliating moment in front of Aiden's parents and the rest of the restaurant patrons. I make a mad dash for the bathroom before I embarrass myself further.

I take a few minutes to check my makeup and gather my thoughts.

Everything is going well. Aiden's parents are lovely, and I feel like I'm making a good first impression.

When I return, Mr. Thomas is reprimanding Harry. "Harrison, you shouldn't make such a bold move just yet, especially with your track record."

I give Aiden a curious look, and he shakes his head.

"Are you alright?" Mrs. Thomas asks me.

"Yes, thank you."

"Good. Now, Erin, tell me what you do at the magazine. Is it the same work as Bre?" she asks.

I clear my throat. I was hoping my escape to the bathroom would allow everyone time to move past the Bre conversation.

"Um...yes. We're both journalists. I've been with *Strike a Pose* for a few years, and thankfully I've been given carte blanche to choose the topics I write about. I love what I do."

Aiden pretends to give a golf clap, and I punch him on the leg.

"Well, it sounds fascinating," she replies. "Will you have the same opportunity as Bre to work abroad?"

Harry's eyes get wide. I'm sure he's worried that I might throw Bre under the bus. Huh. He must really like her.

Truthfully, I'm torn. I could tell them about the type of person Bre is, and revenge would be so sweet. But I know this isn't the time or place. It's actually an opportunity to show that I'm a better person.

"Erin had the chance to go to Paris as well," Aiden interrupts. "But she's extremely loyal to *Strike a Pose* and has been working very hard to promote within our magazine here. I've seen some of her work, and it's spectacular. I see a huge future here in San Francisco, and personally, I'm happy she didn't go to Paris."

Aiden reaches over and gives my hand a squeeze. If I wasn't falling in love with him before, I am now.

Meanwhile, Harry's shoulders relax thanks to Aiden's explanation and me not revealing Bre's true colors.

"It sounds like our boys have impeccable taste," Mr. Thomas exclaims. "They got that from me."

Mrs. Thomas beams.

Thankfully there's no more mention of my job, Bre, or Paris. As the dinner conversation continues, my mind keeps replaying everything Aiden said. I love that he believes in me and my work.

"What are you thinking about?" Aiden whispers, pulling me out of my daydream. "You were staring off into space."

"I'm just happy to be here," I whisper back.

He gently rubs my arm.

I can understand why this restaurant has such a fantastic reputation. The food is unbelievable, and the wine is even better. Actually, the wine is probably too good. I think everyone is a little buzzed by the end of the meal. Harry and Aiden get into an argument about who was a better soccer player ten years ago, and their parents are sharing stories from when they started dating.

"Erin, how long have your parents been married?" Mrs. Thomas asks.

I completely freeze. This would be another topic I'd rather not discuss.

"My parents? Oh…um…forty years."

This isn't a lie. They were married forty years before they divorced, and since they're now getting remarried, I don't know if their time apart counts or not.

"Actually, it's kind of complicated," I add. "My parents were married for forty years, but they divorced two years ago."

Mrs. Thomas gives me an apologetic look. "Oh, I'm sorry for being so presumptuous."

"No, please don't," I say, holding up my hand. "In a bizarre twist, my parents just announced that they're getting remarried. Apparently they needed a break or something. To be honest, I don't really understand any of it."

"They're getting remarried on a cruise ship, and they've invited me," Aiden tells them.

Aiden's parents look confused, and I don't blame them. I'm still completely lost when it comes to my parents' unconventional relationship, although it'll be nice to have my family back together again.

"Aiden made quite an impression on my family," I say, giving him a wink. "You raised a great man."

"They sure did," Harry exclaims, holding up his wine glass. "Me."

Aiden rolls his eyes. "You wish, bro."

"I'd like to make a toast," Harry continues, ignoring his brother. "To the most influential, loving, and patient people who raised an awesome son and Aiden, too."

We all cheer, while the Thomas's lovingly look at each other and share a sweet kiss. Watching them together makes me feel a bit emotional—they're obviously still very much in love.

As we're leaving the restaurant, Mrs. Thomas gives me a hug. "I hope that we'll be seeing you again, Erin."

I remain calm, but inside I'm ecstatic.

"Thank you. I hope so too."

Aiden gives me a wink before saying good-bye to his parents and Harry.

He doesn't let go of my hand as we make our way back to my apartment.

"I should probably get going," he says after walking me to my front door. I nod even though I don't want him to leave. He leans in to kiss me good-bye.

"Do you want to hang out for a bit?"

He smiles. "I thought you'd never ask."

Once again, the phone rings at five thirty a.m. My best friend and I really need to have a chat about the importance of time zones.

"What?" I mumble when I answer.

"Um, hello. French Laundry? I waited up to hear about your enchanted evening and what do I get in return? Nothing. No call or text. I'm assuming you have a good reason?"

Do I ever. But considering it's so early, I'd rather share every detail after I've had more sleep.

"How about I call you back when it's not the middle of the night?" I beg.

She lets out a frustrated sigh. "I've been up for hours."

Seriously?

"Mia, have you forgotten that Eastern Standard Time and Pacific Standard Time are different—as in three hours different?"

"Nonsense," she exclaims. "You've already left me hanging long enough. I'm on the edge of my seat. Even Jack wants to know what happened."

I groan. I'm sure Jack has much more important things to think about other than my personal life.

This is classic Mia behavior. She calls me early, gets me fired up, and keeps me on the phone until I'm awake. Once again, her grand plan works.

"When did you tell Jack that you were in love with him?" I ask.

I must catch her completely off guard because she doesn't say a word for a few seconds. "Why?"

"Just curious," I say nonchalantly.

She screams so loudly I pull the phone away. "Erin Taylor's in love."

"Ha, ha. Anyway, I'm not planning on telling him yet. I was just wondering."

"Let it happen naturally," she says. "I'm sure he'll say it first."

"Well, assuming he feels the same way," I remind her.

"He feels the same way," she insists. "I just know it."

I curl up under my blanket and smile. *I hope so.*

Chapter Eighteen

I feel like a different person. I'm not sure if the new me is because I'm in love or because I love my job right now. I've been so busy; I haven't turned on the TV in days. Could it be that I've overcome my TV addiction after all these years? Of course this may change as soon as the new season of Emily in Paris comes out. For now, I'll have to live vicariously through *Emily* until I take my own trip to the city of lights. And I will get there someday without anyone's interference.

"Erin, are you listening to me?" my mom snaps. I'm having lunch with her and Liza, and I keep zoning off. It's been nonstop wedding talk since I sat down.

"Of course," I lie.

"You didn't answer my question. What do you think of these dresses?"

My mom has become a complete bridezilla. I never imagined that I'd be a bridesmaid in my parents' wedding, but my mother has decided she wants to bring some tradition to her shotgun cruise ship wedding. She claims that forty years ago they didn't have everything she wanted, although judging from the pictures, it looked pretty grand to me.

"I chose pink and turquoise," she says. "Those colors are very tropical, don't you think? And what about the style? Do you like it?"

I look at the picture Liza is holding up. "They're really pretty, Mom. I'm fine with whatever you decide."

I chew on a piece of bread while she and Liza discuss shoes. My mother is torn between heals and flip flops. I guess I shouldn't complain because her wedding plans have taken precedence over discussing my life.

"Eric will be calling Aiden to discuss their arrangements," Liza tells me. "Your brother really likes Aiden."

I give her a confused look. "What arrangements?"

And why is my brother calling Aiden?

"The arrangements for the suit fittings," Liza replies. She and Mom look at each other. Fittings? What is she talking about?

"Honey, you know Aiden will need to match Eric for the pictures," my mother says. "And little Knox will look so adorable in his little outfit."

Matching outfits?

I thought this was going to be a quaint little vow ceremony with the ship's captain. Now my boyfriend will be twinning with my brother and nephew.

Although this is my mother we're talking about. I shouldn't be surprised by anything she does.

My mother gives me a confused look. "Erin, we can't leave Aiden out. He would be incredibly offended if we didn't ask him to stand beside your father and Eric," she exclaims. "Most importantly, that man loves *you,* so I'm sure he'd do anything for your mother."

I open my mouth to say something, but nothing comes out. Did she just say that Aiden loves me? Is this some kind of mother's intuition...or is it wishful thinking on her part?

"Mom, you don't know that."

She lets out a frustrated sigh. "Erin Marjorie Taylor, I know love when I see it, and that man loves you." She looks at Liza, who's nodding her head in agreement.

I chew on my lower lip. For once I hope my mother's right when it comes to my love life.

"Erin, I've been so impressed by you lately," Chelsie says, handing me another cup of the world's best coffee. "Not that you haven't impressed me in the past, but lately there's something different. I'm not sure what it is exactly—a spark or a newfound confidence. Whatever it is, it's good."

I sit up straighter and hold my head high. I'm so glad she's noticed because I've been trying very hard to stand out since everything went down with the Paris project.

"Now when am I going to see this article you've been raving about?"

"Don't you mean articles?" I suggest, the corner of my mouth turning up. "Inspiration has struck, and my article has become a series."

Chelsie's face lights up.

"Series of articles, huh?" she says thoughtfully. "I'm intrigued. You must really want your own office."

I laugh. "Yes. Very much."

"I suppose it does get kind of crowded out there on the floor, doesn't it?"

Ha. She has no idea. Bre and Aly will be returning from Paris, and all the peace and quiet will be gone in an instant.

"I can understand why you'd want your own space," she says. "You know I try not to listen to the rumors and gossip, but I did hear something about Aiden and Aly. She definitely has a flare for dramatics—certainly different than the timid girl who first started here."

I press my lips together. "Yes, very different."

"Well, I wish I could tell you that she's not returning," Chelsie says.

"It's okay."

Admittedly, I was hoping that Aly would irritate Madeline Bufont enough to get fired, or perhaps do well enough to stay in Paris permanently. At this point either option would suffice.

"Anyway, I'm looking forward to reading your new article series. Send them over as soon as they're ready," she says, changing the subject. I completely understand Chelsie's need to stay impartial, and at the same time I know she has my back.

I take the hint and head back to my desk. As soon as I return, I'm met with the most gorgeous bouquet of roses waiting for me.

"These were just delivered," Kimmy squeals. "I wonder who they're from.

My heart begins to pick up speed as I open the card attached.

Please join me for dinner Friday night. Be ready at 6 p.m.

Aiden

I smile and hold the note to my chest.

"Well?" Kimmy asks.

I shrug. "Just a dinner invitation."

"Hmm…it must be a special occasion."

"I'm not sure, but I can't wait to find out." I pick up my phone to send Aiden a response.

I'd love to have dinner with you on Friday night. Thank you for the roses.

I reach over and touch one of the soft petals. My heart is practically pounding out of my chest. I have a feeling Friday is going to be unforgettable.

∽

It's official. I've completed my series of articles, and now I'm crossing my fingers that this project catapults my career to the next level. I've been working nonstop for the past few days, and I'm finally satisfied enough to send them to Chelsie.

The whole office is preparing for the return of the Paris team. Kimmy has made a point of saying that she's not giving up her new desk no matter how livid Bre gets.

Aiden and I have discussed how different everything would be if I had gone to Paris. He actually wants to thank Bre, because this time together has brought us so much closer. I don't know if I'm ready to do that, but I'm definitely not as upset as I was at first.

Apparently, Harry's visit to Paris went very well. I'm sure he and Aiden are hopeful that Bre and I can bury the hatchet before we all gather together with their parents. Of course it will take some time to build up that trust with Bre, but perhaps we can move forward and co-exist.

Aly is a different story. It will take some time for me to forget her futile attempts to come between me and Aiden.

It's Friday night, and I'm anxiously waiting for Aiden to pick me up for our date. He's been pretty secretive as to the location despite me asking over and over again. The only hint he gave was for me to dress warmly. There's a knock at six o'clock sharp.

I open the door to find Aiden looking as handsome as ever in his dark denim jeans and light blue sweater.

"Hi," I say trying to tone down my excitement.

"Hello, beautiful lady. Would you like to go out with me tonight?"

He takes my face in his hands and gently touches my lips with his. I'm so mesmerized that it takes me a few seconds to open my eyes.

"Are you ready?" he whispers.

I nod slowly as I grab my bag.

"Are you finally going to tell me where we're going?" I ask as soon as we get in the car.

He raises his eyebrows. "Well, I wanted to surprise you, but it's a bit of a drive, so I'm sure you'll figure it out."

I look out the window. We're driving away from the city, but I'm still not sure where we're headed.

As we drive further away from the city, it doesn't take me long to figure out that Aiden is taking me back to the Bristow Winery, the spot of our first date. I can't think of anything more perfect.

"We're going back to the Bristow Winery," I say knowingly.

A big grin spreads across his face. "We'll see."

Sure enough, we arrive at the site of our first date. Aiden parks, and I take a few deep breaths as I wait for him to come to my side of the car. I couldn't be more ready for our magical evening.

Once again, Aiden has outdone himself with the perfect meal, delicious wine, and chocolate-covered strawberries. I feel like the luckiest woman in the world.

While we eat, Aiden tells me about my brother calling him with wedding details.

"I'm so sorry," I say, making a face. "You probably didn't expect to be caught up in a bunch of wedding plans after one dinner with my family. Believe me, I'm still trying to make sense of it myself."

He waves his hand. "I think it's great. I like your family a lot."

I lean my head to the side. "I'll remind you of that after you're around my brother for longer than a few hours."

All of a sudden, he starts fidgeting.

"Is something wrong?"

"I'll be right back." He gets up quickly, and I watch as he rushes around the corner.

I'm so confused. I wait a few minutes, and just as I'm about to search for him, he returns.

"Sorry, I needed a few minutes to get my thoughts together."

He moves his chair closer to me and sits down

"I really wanted tonight to be special." He nervously runs his hand through his hair. "I thought coming back to the location of our first date would set the stage for what I wanted to say."

He looks terrified. And with him acting so strange, it's making me nervous.

"Everything is perfect," I tell him. "Honestly, we could be watching TV at your place, and I'd be happy just being with you."

He holds my hand firmly in his. "I know, but what I'm trying to say is...I'm in love with you. I have been since the first night we came here." He exhales loudly as if he just unloaded a huge weight that had been sitting on his shoulders.

Tears begin to fill my eyes. This is so surreal, and after wanting this for so long, it almost feels like a dream.

"I love you, too," I say, my voice barely above a whisper. I'm unsuccessful at holding back the tears that are in my eyes. "Except I think I fell in love with you long before our first date."

A huge smile spreads across his face.

"It probably started when you gave me that annoying nickname."

He laughs and pulls me into his lap. "I can't tell you how happy I am to hear you say those words. After everything that's happened and how bad I messed up, I wasn't sure if you'd even want me in your life."

I put my finger to his lips. "Don't even think that. My life is better with you in it."

He takes my chin in his hands and kisses me with more urgency than ever before.

I rest my head on his shoulder. "So, you never told me what your parents thought of me," I ask him. "You already know how my family feels. I actually think my mom has a bit of a crush on you. If she wasn't remarrying my dad, you might have something to worry about."

Aiden raises his eyebrows. "An older woman? Hmm..."

I cringe. "Very funny."

He chuckles. "My parents thought you were great. And your mom is a nice lady, but I'm no longer available." He links his fingers with mine. "I don't know what else to say, ET, except the best is yet to come."

Chapter Nineteen

I open my eyes to the sun streaming through the opening of my curtains. I roll over and pull the covers to my chin. I don't think I could be any happier, especially after my unforgettable evening with Aiden. I can't wait to see what the future holds for us and my career at *Strike a Pose*.

Speaking of work life, I've decided that when Bre returns I'll try my best to make amends and move forward. It certainly seems like we'll be in each other's lives one way or another. There's no way to avoid her, considering we work together, and our boyfriends are brothers. I don't expect us to be friends, but we can be cordial with one other for Aiden and Harry. There's also a chance that she won't be too pleased with my series of articles. It's not about her exactly, but I was inspired by my recent experiences.

My phone buzzes from my nightstand, and I quickly reach for it.

Good morning. I love you.

A huge grin spreads across my face when I read Aiden's text. I can't think of a better way to start my day.

~

"Why does it feel like eight weeks have flown too quickly?" Kimmy mutters.

This is the current vibe in the office. It's safe to say that Aly and Bre haven't been missed. Even though I intend to coexist with Bre, I'd much rather her be on the other side of the world. As far as Aly goes, I have no intention of having any kind of relationship with her. We will just be two journalists who work at *Strike a Pose*.

Kimmy and have grown a lot closer since she moved to Bre's desk. Maybe this is another reason I was meant to stay here. We've always gotten along, but Bre demands so much attention that I never had a chance to really get to know Kimmy.

"Should we make welcome back posters for the team?" Kimmy asks, giving me wistful smile. "Or is there such a thing as 'go back to Paris' posters?"

I laugh. "We could make them a thing."

Kimmy casually knocks one of Aly's stuffed dogs off her desk. We watch as the poor stuffed animal sails across the room. I start to giggle and don't even notice Chelsie standing next to my desk watching us.

"Are you girls having fun?" she asks, cracking a smile.

"Yes," I say.

"Always," Kimmy adds.

"Good," Cheslie says. "Erin, stop by my office when you get a chance."

I nod my head. I wonder if she finished reading my articles.

"That seemed rather cryptic," Kimmy says, her voice low.

I grit my teeth. "I sent over the article I've been working on, so I'm assuming that she wants to talk about it."

I don't waste any time heading to Chelsie's office.

She's typing something on her laptop. "Erin Taylor, finally."

What does that mean? She only asked me to come in here a few minutes ago.

"Finally what?" I ask, cautiously.

"I've been waiting for you to send me a piece like this for a while. I'm not sure what has happened, but it seems like you've suddenly come alive." She pauses. "Not that your work hasn't been great in the past, but this is exceptional.

Relief washes over me as I sink down into the chair across from her desk.

"And you'll be happy to know that I've been thinking about your request. Given your time at this magazine and the unfortunate situation with the Paris project, I'm having one of the smaller offices cleaned out for you." She pauses. "It's basically a storage closet, but it's a start."

My mouth drops open. "That's perfect, amazing. Thank you, Chelsie."

She holds up her hand. "It may be only temporary. But I think it will be a good transition for the next few weeks at least."

"I understand. I'm beyond grateful," I gush. "And I'm committed to writing more articles like this one. My creativity has been sparked, and the ideas are flowing."

"Well, at least you had some good inspiration for this piece."

I smile. "Yes, I did."

She holds up a printed copy. "'Friends ForNever.' Genius."

"Very impressive, ET," Aiden calls from the doorway of my new office-closet.

Chelsie worked her magic and within two days, I'm setting up my desk. She says she's waiting on the approval as far as an official promotion, but I don't care. Having my own space to focus and write has already done wonders for my motivation. I feel like a new level of creativity has been unlocked, and I can't wait to get started.

"It's fantastic, isn't it?" I squeal.

"Yes, nice," he says moving towards me and holding his arms out to me.

I hold up my hand to stop him.

"Nope. Not in the office."

We've made a point to remain professional and keep our relationship outside the office. And Aiden has requested to not be a part of any more interview panels if possible.

He pouts. "I don't know about this promotion thing. How am I supposed to flirt with my girlfriend now that she's a big shot with a fancy office?"

"Very funny, Mr. Thomas. You'll just have to save it for after hours."

He moves closer to me and whispers in my ear. "I plan on it."

His warm breath on my neck sends shivers down my spine.

He slowly moves away from me. "See you later?"

"Absolutely."

As soon as he walks out of my office, I sit down in my chair and spin around. Dreams do come true.

There are many things I dislike, but dress fittings have to be at the top of my list. I'm at the bridal shop trying on my bright pink bridesmaid dress. My mom is dancing around the shop, drinking champagne like a newly engaged woman. Honestly, you'd think the woman was getting married for the first time. It's only been a few weeks since my parents announced their re-marriage, but as my mother says there's no time to waste.

"That dress looks like it was made especially for you," she says, holding up her glass.

"Thanks, Mom," I say, staring at myself in the mirror. It's actually not bad at all. My mother does have very good taste.

She sits down in one of the gold wingback chairs. "Sharon and the girls want to do a special ladies' night for me. Do you think it's inappropriate for me to have a bachelorette party?" she asks, pouring herself another glass of champagne. "I'm technically still a bachelorette since I'm divorced, right?"

A bachelorette party? Who is this woman?

"I think dinner with your friends would be fun," I suggest. "That's not technically a bachelorette party."

She gives me a confused look. "But it could be with the right activities."

I know better than to argue with her, so I tell her what she wants to hear. As strange as this is, I can't remember the last time I saw my mom this happy and excited. Maybe my parents needed time apart to realize they were meant to be together.

"By the way, Sharon told me that Wilbur is dating someone and apparently they're getting pretty serious. Of course, I told her about Aiden and how wonderful he is."

I pour myself a glass of champagne and take a sip. "I already know about Will's girlfriend. He told me he was seeing someone when you and Sharon were attempting to play matchmaker."

She gives me a blank stare.

"Anyway," she says, ignoring my comment. "Sharon made a

comment about them getting engaged. I told her that I was expecting Aiden to propose to you at some point too."

I exhale loudly. I shouldn't be surprised that she's turned my personal life into a competition with her friend.

"Mom, please promise that you won't try to rush this," I beg. "Aiden and I are in a good place, and we're happy."

"Helloooo," Liza calls, as she saunters into the shop. She looks fantastic as usual in her skinny jeans and black blazer. "I have shoes."

My mom rushes to her and grabs the bags. I watch them squeal each time they open a box. I'm really glad that my mom has Liza. She loves a good wedding and everything that goes into planning it. I feel slightly guilty that I haven't immersed myself into my parents second wedding.

"Erin, do you want to try on your shoes?" Mom asks, holding up the box.

"Sure, I'd love too."

As expected, Liza's taste is on point. The nude wedges look great with my pink dress.

"Liza, thanks for your input for my article. My boss loved it."

I interviewed Liza and Mia for the Friends ForNever series because I wanted different accounts of friendships, and both of them gave me some great material to use in addition to my own experiences. Talking to them reminded me that all friendships have challenges and go through ups and downs. And sometimes they don't last forever.

"I'm so glad," she says. "I really enjoyed it."

"Liza, I was just telling Erin what Sharon told me about Wilbur."

"Will," I interject.

"Oh, right," she says, waving her hand. "Anyway, don't you agree that it would be lovely to get a see another engagement in the near future?"

Liza looks back and forth between my mother and me. I know she doesn't want to say the wrong thing. Liza is a people pleaser.

"Well." She pauses. "I think you and Aiden look great together, and your chemistry is very obvious." She cracks a smile. "I guess anything can happen, right?"

"That's true. You never know."

Even though my mom consumes several glasses of champagne, I make her promise not to bring up engagements or wedding plans to Aiden. I'm not very confident that she'll keep her promise, but hopefully she'll be too preoccupied with her own upcoming marriage to worry about my life.

I've been so busy with my parents' wedding plans, Aiden, and the endless story ideas that the day we've all been dreading has snuck up on me. The Paris team returns today, and Kimmy is still upset that I left her in the trenches with Bre and Aly. None of us know what to expect, but I'm expecting plenty of comments that begin with "When I lived in Paris" or "I came up with the most brilliant idea while I was walking along the Seine."

When I arrive at the office, Chelsie is the only person there. I barge into her office and sit down. She looks at me, shakes her head, and starts laughing.

I roll my eyes. "What?"

"A little on edge, are we?" she asks.

"Just a tad. Things were super awkward the last time we saw each other."

"I have a feeling that everything will be fine," she says knowingly. "And if not, you can escape to your office and write about it."

I laugh. "Is that your way of telling me to get to work?"

"Subtly."

As soon as I step out of Chelsie's office, Aly is standing there. This has to be one of the most awkward moments I've ever experienced.

"Hello, Aly."

"Erin," she says coldly.

She walks past me into Chelsie's office and immediately starts raving about her experience at *Bleu Amour*. She's practically yelling, which I'm sure is for my benefit. I sigh. Let the fun begin.

When I return to my office, I open my laptop. I made the mistake of telling my mom to email me about wedding stuff instead of calling or texting. After scrolling through my emails, I'm regretting that decision. She also gave my email address to Sharon, who's now sending me emails titled *Margie's Bachelorette*

Party, Taking it back to the Old School. I really wish I didn't open any of those because there are certain things you can't unsee. I may have to skip this party—or potentially be scarred for life.

I'm startled by a knock. When I turn around, I find Bre standing in the doorway. Neither of us says anything at first until she walks in and sits down.

"I see you finally got your office. Congrats."

"Thanks. Welcome back," I say, sitting up straight.

"You may not be ready to talk, but I wanted to apologize again. I wish I could take everything back."

I'm sure she's trying to be sincere, but this is Bre we're talking about. She did what she had to do to get what she wanted.

"What's done is done. Let's just try to move forward the best we can."

She gives me a curious look. "So, we can move forward? For Harry and Aiden, of course."

I knew she'd bring them up, and she does have a point.

"Yes," I agree. I'm not sure what else to say. It'll probably take a while before we sit down over coffee or drinks and discuss her fabulous two months in Paris.

"Thank you, Erin," she says, rising to her feet.

After she leaves, Kimmy comes in and folds her arms. "I may never forgive you for leaving me alone out there. Aly is the worst, and the stint in Paris has turned her into a monster. She hasn't stopped running her mouth all morning."

Poor Kimmy.

"I'm sorry," I say with a frown. "I have a pair of headphones you can use."

She dramatically throws her head back. "I'm determined to up my writing game," she says, pounding her fist on my desk. "I need one of these offices."

"Go for it," I exclaim.

On my way home, I pick up Chinese food for Aiden and me. I love our evenings together. I'm feeling really positive about my life right now, and everything seems to be falling into place.

Today turned out to be much better than I expected. I know I'll have to interact with Aly at some point, but I'll just have to take things one day at a time.

My friendship with Bre is different. Aiden is right—I probably should be thanking her because it turned out to be a blessing in disguise that I didn't go to Paris.

As soon as Aiden arrives, he engulfs me in his arms for what seems like several minutes. I don't think I'll ever get tired of this kind of greeting.

While we're having dinner, Aiden and I talk about the return of the Paris team.

"Truthfully, I'm glad today's over." I lean back on the couch. "And as awkward as it was, I feel rejuvenated tonight. It's almost like their return has given me closure. That probably sounds weird."

He pushes a stray strand of hair behind my ear. "Not at all, considering how things were when they left."

"Exactly."

"But, speaking of weird, I received a phone call from your mom today."

I groan. I can't believe my mother is calling my boyfriend. I hope she didn't say anything embarrassing, but I know better.

"Lovely," I exclaim.

He laughs. "Don't worry. We only talked for about an hour or so."

"An hour?" I shout. "What could Mama Margie talk about for an hour? And don't tell me it was all about her wedding."

He reaches over and puts his finger to my lips.

"Oh there was plenty of talk about her wedding, her friends, and her bachelorette party. And then a bit of inquiring about my future plans."

I cringe. I knew she wasn't going to keep her promise. It'll probably get even worse after her wedding is over.

"She never stops," I tell him. "I actually thought her cruise wedding would distract her enough from meddling in my personal life. Wishful thinking, of course."

He laughs.

"Believe it or not, I enjoy talking to her. She entertains me, and she's good for my ego."

"Yes, I still believe she has a crush on you."

"Can you blame her?" he asks, giving me a wink.

I place my hand on his cheek. "Not a bit."

He takes my hand and kisses it. "Erin, I love your family, and I love you. I can't remember ever being this happy, and I told your mother that."

Tears begin to fill my eyes, and one escapes down my cheek. Aiden gently wipes it away with his finger.

"I also told Margie that I'm really excited for what our future holds and I have some pretty big plans."

My heart starts to pound against the wall of my chest.

"Big plans? And what do those include, Mr. Thomas."

He shrugs nonchalantly. "You'll just have to wait and see, ET. It's going to be pretty epic, though."

I lean in to kiss him. "I can't wait."

This is what life is all about. Not my mother, our crazy families, Bre, Harry, or Aly. Just Aiden and I spending time together and dreaming about the future.

"So, do you want to watch some TV?" Aiden asks, holding up the remote.

I shake my head. "Nah, tonight is perfect just the way it is."

"I couldn't agree more."

Epilogue

I shouldn't be this stressed out—this isn't my wedding, and my parents have been married before. We leave in three days, and my mom has us all running around doing last minute errands in preparation for this wedding cruise. She has truly morphed into a complete bridezilla over the past few months. Honestly, you'd think this was her first marriage, not a second marriage to a man she was married to for forty years. Sometimes I wonder if she got divorced so she could have a do-over on the wedding. Crazier things have happened.

I'm still trying to recover from my mother's bachelorette party, which was last weekend. I knew I would regret going, and I do. It was like going clubbing with the Golden Girls, except definitely not as fun. Sharon went out of her way to research bachelorette parties and implemented all the novelty trimmings. I'm not sure I'll forget it without a bit of therapy.

Even with all the craziness, the most awkward part of the night was when Sharon unloaded on me about what a great catch Will is and how I should only be so lucky to have a man like him. I bit my tongue, but she was pretty relentless for about five minutes. It wasn't until she decided to do a body shot off the bouncer that she stopped lecturing me. Yes, that's an image I can't seem to get out of my mind.

Liza also let loose and divulged too much information about her and Eric's private life. I don't understand why everyone feels the need to share their deepest, darkest secrets with me. I have no interest in knowing certain things about my parents or my brother. I only had one glass of wine because someone had to be the responsible adult.

Aiden was lucky enough to enjoy a peaceful fishing trip down the coast with Eric, my dad, and a few friends. Aiden and Eric are quickly becoming besties. I don't get it, but Aiden continuously reminds me that he grew up with Harry. As irritating as my brother can be, I appreciate that he's been so welcoming to Aiden.

Mia continues to call me at five thirty a.m. at least twice a week. She says time zones don't matter when you are life-long best friends—and maybe she's right. She invited Aiden and me to Florida to visit now that we're officially serious enough to take a vacation together. My parents' surprise wedding cruise pushed us over that line. When I asked Aiden if he wanted to go to Miami, he was all for it. We're planning a trip over the holidays, and I can't wait to see my best friend and meet her dream man, Jack. I mean, who doesn't want to meet a Hemsworth brother look-alike? Except for Aiden—he's definitely not as excited to meet him as I am. Ever since I referred to Jack as a marvel superhero look-alike, he's been in the gym every day.

Chelsie has been very supportive of my upcoming trips considering I've never taken a vacation in all my years at the magazine. Looking back, I have no idea why I didn't take any time off. It's time for me to start enjoying my life.

I'm sure it doesn't hurt that my "Friends ForNever" articles are really picking up momentum. I guess everyone can relate to stories of friendship, relationship conflict, and resolution. It reminds us that we're not alone despite feeling that way at times.

According to Chelsie, I've single-handedly brought new life into the magazine. Hearing this has restored my faith in myself, and I'm hoping it leads to more inspired writing.

As I expected, Bre wasn't exactly happy when she found out about the articles and the fact that I included some personal experience. Of course I didn't mention any names, but I'm sure it was a reminder of how she wasn't originally chosen to go to Paris.

In her defense, I've seen a lot of change in her since she's been back. She's still the same old Bre, but there are signs of a new and improved person who cares about people other than herself.

Aly and I don't speak, and I'm perfectly content with that. She knows she's basically alone on the island, and the only people who communicate with her on a regular basis are Chelsie and Sean. This is mostly because she now thinks she's superior to everyone in the office after being in Paris. There's a rumor that Aly and Sean had a thing when they were overseas, but she blew him off as soon as they came back to the states. Aly has her sights set on a big future, and I don't think she's going to let anything get in her way.

I actually hope she gets what she wants, or rather what she deserves. I did hear that she ended up making a good impression on the powers that be at *Bleu Amour*, including Madeline Bufont. I'm pretty sure Aly is here to stay, and that means we'll be working together for the foreseeable future.

Harry and Bre are getting more serious by the day, and Aiden thinks he's going to propose to her. Last week we had our first family dinner all together since Bre returned from Paris.

As usual, Bre went overboard trying to impress everyone. She monopolized most of the conversation talking about Paris. I had to count to ten and takes some deep breaths when she said, "Erin, you absolutely need to go to France one day."

Just when I started to enjoy myself, Mrs. Thomas apologized for missing my mother's bachelorette party. I had no idea she'd been invited. Thankfully she wasn't able to attend.

Much to my dismay, there are pictures floating around social media of the party. It turns out Sharon is one of those people on Facebook who befriends everyone she meets, and their friends. I had to block her from tagging me in pictures from the party.

In addition to the party invite, my mother invited Aiden's parents to join us on the wedding cruise next week. They had to decline due to a prior engagement, and I couldn't be more relieved. I know they'll all meet at some point, but thankfully it won't be on a boat at my parents second wedding.

My mother continues to drop hints about Aiden and I getting engaged. I know she's in a mad rush for it to happen before Will proposes to his girlfriend, and it's so frustrating. Sharon and her seem to have a never-ending competition thing going on.

This reminded me that friendships are hard work no matter what age you are. There will be disagreements, heartbreak, competition, and jealousy between even the closest of friends.

I've learned that there will be times friends hurt and disappoint you. But there will be more moments when friends uplift and support you. Everything that I've been through, good and bad, has brought me to this point in my life. And although friends have come and gone, I know now that they were the friends for never. I've accepted that I'm ready to move forward and focus on how lucky I am to have people in my life who will be my friends forever.

THE END

Dear Reader

I hope you enjoyed *Friends ForNever.* Please take a few minutes to leave a review on Amazon.

Want a Free Short Story? Click here.
Love my books? Join my reader tribe on Facebook!

Visit my website for updates, and stay tuned for my next book coming soon.

Can We Talk? Now Available

Buy the first book in the Question series or read with your Kindle Unlimited Membership!

Can We Talk? The last time I heard these words, my relationship ended. Though it was mutual, it hasn't stopped me from spending countless sleepless nights overthinking all the what-ifs.

Inspired by a life coach, I, Eliza Hawkes, realize it's time to make some changes in my life. I'm ready to face my journey head-on, but just as I take a step forward, my cousin drops a bombshell.

Recovering from the shocking news will be hard, but thankfully there's a distraction in the chaos. My best friend and perpetual bachelor, Mason, begs me to attend a quick weekend getaway to New York City, all at his company's expense. The only thing we need to do is pretend to be in a relationship. This should be easy, considering Mason's been my ride-or-die for years.

What I don't plan for is the weekend to take such an unexpected turn, leaving me shaken to my core. The effects of which could have a lasting impact. It's time for Mason and me to have a very important talk. But am I ready to take this leap of faith and risk losing the most important thing in my life, or would it be better if everything stayed the same?

From USA Today bestselling author Melissa Baldwin comes a brand new swoony story that will give you all the feels.

About the Author

USA Today bestselling author Melissa Baldwin always dreamed of sharing her stories with the world. She brought this vision to life, becoming an award-winning, bestselling author of over thirty romantic comedies and cozy mysteries. Melissa is also a wife, mother, new empty-nester, and travel advisor.

Her books feature charming, ambitious, and real women, whom she considers part of her tribe. Although she rarely takes a day off, when she's not writing, she enjoys quality time with her family, traveling, attempting yoga poses, and booking Disney vacations. Melissa still uses a paper planner, and her guilty pleasures include Beverly Hills 90210 reruns and General Hospital.

Made in the USA
Monee, IL
08 January 2026

41207611R00154